Go to the House of Berber!

Larry & Margaret Rogers' Story

By

Ravonne Green, Ph.D.

XUlon PRESS

Go to the House of Berber!
Larry & Margaret Rogers' Story
by Ravonne Green, Ph.D.

Printed in the United States of America

ISBN 9781626979161

Unless otherwise indicated, Bible quotations are taken from The New International Version of the Bible. Copyright © 1985 by Zondervan.

www.xulonpress.com

TABLE OF CONTENTS

❧

DEDICATION

I would like to dedicate this book to the memory of my uncle, Larry Rogers. Uncle Larry served the Lord faithfully as a pastor in the Appalachian Conference and as a missionary of World Missions Ministries of the International Pentecostal Holiness Church. He was never too tired or too busy to serve the needs of others. He prayed fervently and worked diligently to advance the kingdom of Christ in any way that he could.

I would also like to dedicate this book to my aunt, Margaret Rogers, who served faithfully with Uncle Larry in all of his endeavors. The Lord called them as a team in ministry from the early years of their ministry. She was as committed to prayer and to service as Uncle Larry and worked faithfully by his side to accomplish God's work. She fought with him in his battle against cancer and rejoiced with him when the battle ended and he went to his final reward on January 18, 2012.

Most importantly, I would like to dedicate this book to the glory of God who does all things well. May we all be inspired by those who have gone before us to fight the good fight and to finish the race.

Ravonne Green, Ph.D.

ACKNOWLEDGEMENTS

The author gratefully acknowledges the following individuals for their assistance in preparing this work. This work would not have been possible without their contributions.

Chapter 1- Everett Joseph Rogers, Jr., Doyle Rogers, and Mary Francis Webb-materials about the Rogers family and early childhood memories about Larry. Bruce & Mary Francis Webb also provided a tour of the Rogers' home place, the Allisonia Pentecostal Holiness Church and other sites that were a part of the Roger's story.

Chapter 2- Marie Hollingsworth, Aileen Collins, Yvonne Green and Jim Bishop; materials about Margaret's early childhood.

Chapter 4- Aileen Collins, Everett Joseph Rogers, Jr., and James Newton-materials about Margaret and Larry's college days.

Chapter 6- De Seawright and John Woodzell-materials about the Mitchelltown Pentecostal Holiness Church.

Chapter 8- The Reverend Billy Griffin-Saint Albans Pentecostal Holiness church history and Jim Bishop.

Chapter 12- Exploratory trip notes-Margaret Rogers.

Chapters 13-15- Marie Hollingsworth correspondence with Margaret.

Margaret Rogers' journal entries, emails and conversations about Morocco

Everett Joseph Rogers, Jr. and Marie Hollingsworth provided many hours of content editorial assistance.

PREFACE

A few months before he passed into the presence of Jesus Christ, my wife and I visited Larry and Margaret Rogers at their home in Dublin, Virginia. Also visiting were Margaret's sister Marie and her husband Winston Hollingsworth (both couples were International Pentecostal Holiness Church missionaries having served on the continent of Africa). Though Larry was visibly weakened in body, his mind was sharp and clear. I asked him his age and with a bit of a protest in his voice declared, "Not old enough!" We all laughed, but I knew he was saying that he wanted to go back to North Africa.

I first met this wonderful couple nearly fifty years ago when, on occasion, I would accompany my father to the camp meetings and annual conference of the then Virginia Conference in Dublin. As a denominational executive, Daddy would sometimes be assigned to preside over the conference. I spent my time in those teenage years making friends with the other teens who came to camp meeting. Some of those friendships remain to this day.

But I distinctly remember this couple that stood out from everyone else. He was handsome, tall, proper and almost debonair. She was, to put it mildly, stunningly beautiful. But even then as a teenager, I could discern a quality about them that reflected a special grace of God. As a teenager, for people like that to speak to you and know your name was a very affirming experience.

As the years went by I came to know them in other roles. I learned from colleagues how Larry reached out to younger ministers with encouragement. He always seemed to know when a younger minister was discouraged or drifting in the call and would take time to visit, listen and give encouragement. The present Bishop of the Appalachian Conference, Reverend Preston Mathena, was one of those young men whose life was guided by the caring focus of Larry Rogers.

As the years went by I heard that after years of faithful pastoral service, Larry and Margaret had heard the voice of God to go to Morocco. The Holy Spirit spoke to Larry in a dream about the Berber people in this North African nation. The challenges were great: Morocco is a Moslem nation and it is a very difficult place to minister. The measures of success we use in the Western world, such as number of congregations and Sunday school attendance, are not useful measurements in such an environment.

In 2005 I was elected as the Executive Director of IPHC World Missions Ministries. In meeting the Rogers in Africa, I found myself wondering why this couple had left comfortable American pastorates. Why, as they approached the years when most people slow down and prepare for retirement, did the Lord send them to such a difficult place?

In talking with them about their missionary service, I discovered the mysterious and wonderful ways of the Lord. Because of their age and glorious white hair, they were respected and honored among the Moslem people of Morocco. There were times when other younger missionaries were forced to leave that nation. But Larry and Margaret were allowed to remain.

They learned Arabic well enough to communicate on the street. They demonstrated Christian love and kindness every day in the market stalls. Little by little the Holy Spirit used them to manifest a different way of life—the life of a citizen of the kingdom of God. The passport of that kingdom is love. As the years rolled by they began to lead people to meet and follow Jesus Christ as Lord of their life.

There were no big celebrations, no public announcements and no campaigns to take the city. It was the beauty of holiness lived out among people. One by one men and women discovered the love of God through this couple.

In many respects it was their age and dignity that were their best assets. The Lord had prepared them through decades of faithful service in the church, school and community. Their calling came to its fullest bloom in those twenty years in Morocco.

In Morocco today there are no church buildings named in honor of Larry and Margaret. There are no schools, no hospitals or clinics in their honor. But people are there whose lives have been changed forever. These people are "living stones" as the Apostle Peter so aptly describes. They are the living memorials to the life and service of Larry and Margaret Rogers in Morocco.

The beauty of this is that there are "living stones" across Virginia, West Virginia, North Carolina and other parts of this world. Because of Larry and Margaret Rogers, these "living stones" make up the most enduring work of all creation, the living church of Jesus Christ!

I pray that this inspiring record will touch all of us with that same willingness to hear God speak to us, regardless of our age.

Doug Beacham
IPHC General Superintendent

INTRODUCTION

This book is the story of a journey, a heritage and a reward. The journey began for the Rogers family when Josiah Fugate Rogers and Sarah Laurence Rogers determined that they would forsake witchcraft, alcohol and violence. Their decision to embrace Christianity and to serve whole-heartedly the true and living God was to change their family and ultimately to reach lost souls around the world.

The journey began for the Bishop family when Jesse and Mabel Bishop walked for miles to the newly formed Asbury Pentecostal Holiness Church in Asbury, North Carolina and dedicated their lives to the Lord's service. Their sacrifices were many in their journey that began as they trudged down the little country road with their five children any time the church doors were open.

The journey of faith was not always easy. These families experienced hardships, sicknesses and untimely deaths. They faced financial difficulties and other struggles, but their faith in God never wavered. Their tenacity and dedication are our heritage.

Both families were known for their musical abilities. When these talents were yielded to the Lord, He gave them a song in their hearts and helped them to lift others spirits as they shared the joy of the Lord in music. Both families produced ministers of the gospel, missionaries and teachers.

Larry and Margaret must have felt somewhat like Moses on the back side of the desert. They knew that God had called them to be missionaries when they were college students, but the opportunity did not come for them to go to a foreign mission field until they retired.

They used each pastoral appointment to prepare them for their ultimate calling. They learned to be resourceful and to tailor their methods to reach different groups of people in this country. They developed skills in agriculture and teaching English as a second language. They saw how that even some of the training that they had received as children prepared them for missionary service.

God's timing was perfect when He sent Larry and Margaret to the Moroccan culture as senior citizens. Senior citizens are respected for their white hair in Morocco. Senior citizens are not typically involved in activities to convert Muslims to Christianity. They are perceived as being less of a threat to the religious and political establishment.

Larry walked around the ancient Medina every morning and prayed for the Muslims. Margaret taught them how to read the scriptures as she taught them English as a second language. They distributed Bibles; they baptized new converts in the bathtub. They fed the hungry and clothed the poor and, so, fulfilled the law of Christ. Only eternity will unveil the reward.

Ravonne Green, Ph.D.

Part I

Early Childhood & College Days

Chapter One

Halsey Laurence Roger's Family Heritage & Early Years

❧

But where sin increased, grace increased all the more, so that, just as sin reigned in death, so also grace, might reign through righteousness to bring eternal life through Jesus Christ our Lord (Romans 5:20).

Halsey Laurence Roger's Family Heritage

Josiah stood squarely in the corn field with his shot gun waiting for Laura to emerge from the house where the church group was meeting. He had told her that if she ever went to that church again that he would shoot her. He was a man of his word. He opened his whiskey bottle and took another drink. He had to do this; he had to prove to her and to everyone else that he was not going to have anything to do with this religion.

Laura finally emerged from the door of the house. He would wait until she got to the cornfield closer to their house. Their house was about a mile up the hollow from the house where the church met. He did not want people to come over from the church group. This was a private family matter. He took another drink. He could hear her singing as she walked. She sang like an angel. He did not see anyone else coming from the house. He carefully aimed for her head and fired the shotgun.

Josiah could not stop shaking. He had not drunk bad whiskey and he had not had a bad dream. This was the most frightening experience of his life. Laura was hovering over him asking what was wrong. She must have thought that he had shot himself. He could not speak; his heart pounded wildly in his chest. Sweat poured from his forehead. He lay on the ground shaking. He had thrown down the shotgun. He could not find the courage to look up. He never deserved to have a wife like Laura. He could not tell her what had happened.

It was some time later before he confessed that the night that he had fired the gun to fatally wound her, an angel had stood in front of her blocking the bullet. He had seen the angel. This incident only added to his misery. He could not understand her religion and he did not want to understand it. He later told this story widely after he was converted.

Josiah Fugate Rogers (Larry's Grandfather)

Unlike his wife, Josiah (Joe) Rogers was not a church-going man. Josiah wanted nothing to do with Christianity. He had been raised in witchcraft and resisted Christianity verbally, violently and viciously.

The relatives said that he was as good as gold when he was sober. He loved his moonshine and when he was soused, he would turn his drunken anger and frustration toward Laura and the children. On one occasion he chased her around the house with a double bit axe. Another time he shot at her with a shotgun, because she was adamant about attending church. The house where they lived became known as the angel house, because the family believed that the Lord had sent angels to protect them from Josiah before he became a Christian.

One time Laura somehow had an intuition that she should get all of the children out of the house. She told Dalene, the oldest daughter, to climb out of a window and she passed her baby through the window to her. As she handed the baby out the window, Josiah appeared with his shotgun.

He later boarded up all of the windows and doors inside so that they could not come back. Laura and the children walked across the hill to their Aunt Maude's house to wait until Josiah's anger subsided. The nail holes are still along the windows where he boarded them shut.

Early one morning at breakfast, when Laura approached Josiah about attending the revival in progress at the local church, he laid down the law. He told her with foul expletives and ungodly adjectives that she would never darken the door of that church again. Ending the conversation in an abrupt manner, he hitched the horses up to a single tree plow and headed back to work in the field. Laura began to pray fervently. That evening when Josiah came back from the field, he asked, "Laura, are you going to church tonight?" She wept and told him that she would not go because he had told her emphatically that she should never go again. He answered, "You get your church clothes on. I'll find something to wear. I'm going to church with you tonight." He went down to the river and got in the boat with her. They crossed the river and passed through the doors of that church that he so hated and he went to the altar that night and surrendered his life to Jesus. He committed the next 26 years of his life to the Lord and was a powerful testimony of the saving grace of God.

He told that when he went out to plow that conviction struck him like a bolt of lightning on that memorable day. He knelt down by his plow and began to plead with God to save his soul. Laura's prayers had apprehended Josiah Rogers.

Sara Laurence (Moore) Rogers (Larry's Grandmother)

Sara Laurence Rogers and her twin sister were born in 1877. Everett's mother, Sara Laurence (Laura) was well known for her nursing ability. She was a midwife and delivered over 60 babies. She also sat with dying people and spoke of "the death rattles", a certain cough that is caused by an accumulation of fluid in the lungs. She spoke of holding the hands of dying people and claiming their souls. She was a prayer warrior and had great faith. Her love and devotion to Christ and her church was the focal point of her life.

Everett Joe Rogers, Sr. (Larry's Father)

Everett Joe Rogers, Sr. was born and raised on a farm in Delton, Virginia at the head waters around thirteen miles above Claytor Lake and Dam. His parents were Josiah Fugate Rogers and Sarah Laurence Moore-Rogers. He and his seven siblings grew up near the old Arbuckle Iron Ore Mine, across the New River from Allisonia, Virginia.[1] The Arbuckle Mine at Delton was named after Arbuckle coffee, according to Everett Rogers, Sr. The iron ore mines at Delton were closed when Everett was born. [2]

Between paydays, the miners would get Arbuckle coffee on credit from the local store. They would use the coffee at the blind tiger in exchange for bootleg liquor. A blind tiger was where someone would put coffee or money into a two-way drawer and receive a bottle of booze in return. The person on either side never saw the other.

There was a building near the Rogers' house called "The Green Fly" where moonshine whiskey was sold. The Rogers family tells about the circuit riding preacher, Robert Sheffy coming there and praying for

God to destroy it. A storm came shortly after Preacher Sheffy's prayer and a huge ancient oak tree fell on The Green Fly and destroyed it. The Rogers' house is still standing.[3]

Delton had two ferries operating at the turn of the century. Dr. Bruce Clark's ferry crossed the river in Delton and Dr. John Clark's ferry crossed in Allisonia.

In 1915 the conservation division stopped the mines from running mud into the river. They closed them all down because iron was discovered in Lake Erie and they claimed that the Arbuncle Iron Ore mine was the source. They said that the iron concentration was so high that you could dip it out with clam shells.

Most of Delton including the road, Jim Rigney's mill and a store were submersed in the Claytor Lake Dam when it was constructed in 1939. The lake was a 4,500 acre project constructed by the Appalachian Power Company to produce electricity for the southwest Virginia area.[4]

The Rogers' home was often the sight of huge family gatherings with brothers, sisters, aunts, uncles, cousins, relatives, friends joshing each other, joking, trading yarns, reviewing memories and singing with the old pump organ and fiddle. Celebrations were complete with homemade ice cream, softball games and enjoying each other's fellowship. There were special days in the summer remembering birthdays, vacationing families and other occasions.

Thanksgiving was a cherished time with genuine thanksgiving for each member of the family and for all of Gods' blessings. Everyone joined in to help their parents with getting ready for another winter.

At Easter, the adults hid eggs for the little ones to hunt. One unusual year their grandmother made the mistake of taking all of the boiled and colored eggs to the church for their hunt and none were left for the grandchildren. Everyone just laughed at the error. Life on the Rogers' farm was much like life on Walton's Mountain. The Rogers were a loving family that stayed in contact and enjoyed visiting relatives and friends.

The Rogers farmed the rich soil, plowing, planting, cultivating, canning and storing the fruits of their labors. There was no electricity and plowing by hand was difficult. They raised cattle, pigs and chickens and turkeys. If one of the children got sick his mother would fry him an egg. A fried egg was a rare treat since the eggs were usually taken to the market and traded for food, clothing and other needs. The smokehouse smelled of curing hams. The corn crib was full of corn drying to be husked and ground to meal to furnish bread for the family and for the pigs and chickens to eat.

Soft down feathers were valuable for pillows and clean straw was reserved for straw tick mattresses. The older boys hid blackberries and other ingredients to make home brew. When their mother found their hiding place, she was quick to pour camphor into the solution to make cold and croup remedies for the winter. Once, she found some blackberries, which were too contaminated for human consumption, so she just threw them out in the back yard. The fowl community devoured the berries while she was working in the house. She later came out and found the birds asleep on their backs. She assumed that the birds were dead. She did not want to miss an opportunity to rescue the feathers for down pillows. When she later returned to the site, she saw many chickens, geese and ducks walking around naked. The family suggested that she should have made union suits for each of them to wear until their feathers grew back.

Mother Rogers learned that some of her sons were playing cards and gambling. She knew that it was pointless to try to talk to them about their gambling. She waited until one night when they were sleeping and quietly confiscated their cards. She took each card and wrote a scripture verse on it. She put the cards back where she had found them. Every night when they went out to play poker, she prayed for them and they saw the scripture verses as they played.

Everett was able to complete only seven years of public school because the family needed him to help on the farm. His education continued after he married Thelma Bishop since she was a school teacher. The Odd Fellows had made it possible for her to attend Radford Normal School, now Radford University, where she had prepared to become a school teacher. She married Everett while teaching at a one room school in Floyd County, Virginia.

Thelma Bishop (Larry's Mother)

Thelma Bishop was born in Radford, Virginia. Her parents were Lula Moore Bishop and Halsey Laurence Bishop. Halsey worked in Radford, Virginia at a pipe shop. Tragedy struck when Thelma was ten years old. The 1918 influenza epidemic claimed the lives of both of her parents, a brother and an uncle in eleven months.[5 and 6]

Just before her mother died, she gave her new baby, Halsey, to her sister who raised him along with her own baby, Harold Morris and the two boys were raised as brothers in Pulaski, Virginia. At age ten, Thelma assumed the role of mother in the family until her father died. None of the relatives were able to take in the other four children, so they were raised at an Odd Fellows Home in Lynchburg, Virginia.

Music, Music, Music

The home in Delton where Larry's father grew up was very musical. They delighted in playing music and participating in barn dancing. Family members played the acoustical guitar, mandolin, harmonica, pump organ and Everett's mother was a left-handed banjo picker. Their music helped to end a hard working day on a merry note.

The Allisonia Pentecostal Holiness Church was established in 1911 just across New River from where the Rogers family lived. Their mother, Sarah Laurence Rogers attended a revival and was gloriously saved at this church. Her Godly influence changed her family. She along with her twin sister walked a mile and sat in a boat, while someone else stood and with a long pole reaching the bottom of the river, pushed the boat across the river and back after service each time the church doors were open.

Mrs. Rogers taught a little card class at the Allisonia Pentecostal Holiness Church during Sunday school for over fifty years. This was a Sunday school class for beginners. The cards would have a picture for the children to color and a lesson for them to read. The children would memorize a scripture verse and sing a children's song pertaining to the lesson.

Laura's oldest daughter became a nurse at a hospital in Marion, Virginia. She married a doctor and the two of them spent most of their lives in the medical profession in Thurmont, Maryland.

Everett was trained as a male attendant and worked at the Southwestern State Hospital in Marion (Southwestern Virginia Mental Health Institute). He left saying that it was too much for him to have to get a patient in a secure position with his head between his legs and give him a spinal tap with a needle the size of a ten-penny nail. Since Everett was quite a prankster, it is debatable as to whether he was just joking. He asked if the children had ever heard of the Dead Sea. When he got an affirmative answer, he was rapid and proud to relate that his father had shot it. He described situations in which patients would pick up a set of steel bed springs and throw them at him; he had to back through a door to keep the springs from hitting him. Everett left the hospital in Marion to become a mechanic.

Marriage

Everett married Thelma Bishop and they moved to the West Virginia coalfields. The Rogers' moved to the Carter Coal Company Mining Camp in Saw Mill Holler at Six, near Coalwood, West Virginia.[7]

Everett and Thelma were musicians and they played for card parties, dances and festivities in the community. Everett played the guitar and Thelma picked the mandolin. Shortly after they moved to Six, a stranger knocked at the door and asked if they made music. When they said, "Yes," the stranger said, "Mr. Rogers, I am going to preach a revival down at the old school house. Would you come and make music?"

They accepted Pastor Lawson's invitation and they never played for another beer party. The Holy Spirit accomplished His plan and the Rogers were converted. Everett's mother's prayers were no doubt influential in this event. Only eternity will reveal the full impact of their decision to follow Christ. Everett and Thelma Rogers did their best to shape and mold the lives of their family and to encourage them to be a part of the Body of Christ.

Larry's father became a deacon and Sunday school teacher and his mother served as the song leader. Larry and both of his brothers devoted their lives to the ministry, following the example of these two Godly parents who did not send the boys to church, but took them each time the church doors were open. The Rogers family formed a singing group. Joe who was two years younger than Larry spent his life as a musician and minister of music and taught music in the public schools. Doyle (Laddie, two years younger than Joe, still at the time of this writing) pastors a Church of God congregation in Shippensburg, Pennsylvania.

Reviewing the Foundations

No one knows much more than simple facts about Gary #10, where Larry was born. It was the birth place of the late Bishop Joseph H. Synan. There is a Pentecostal Holiness Church there that has been active for many years. Gary #10, West Virginia and Six, West Virginia are so named because of the enormous fans that are located in those areas, supplying ventilation to the mines so that underground workers will not be subjected to the buildup of toxic gases that can explode and cause tunnels to cave in and kill miners, or cause them to suffocate.

The Gauley Bridge disaster In 1936 precipitated mining safety reforms. This disaster occurred when workers were drilling a tunnel for a hydroelectric plant at Gauley Bridge, West Virginia. 476 workers died and 1,500 workers were permanently disabled when they inhaled the dust from the rock in this area, which contained high silica concentrations. Medical experts and engineers were called in to develop methods for reducing the dangers of silica and other substances that miners were exposed to in their work. They developed a film; *Stop Silicosis.*[9] This movie was shown nationwide to prevent similar disasters in other mines and highway engineering projects.

Halsey Laurence (Larry) Rogers was born in Gary #10 West Virginia on May 22, 1929. He was the first son. Everett Joseph (Joe) Rogers, the second son, was born in Saw Mill Hollow in Six, West Virginia on November 18, 1931 in a little four room coal camp house. It had an outside toilet many steps down from the back porch, across a wooden bridge and over in the hillside behind the house.

Their third son, James Douglas Rogers, was born on June 23, 1933. Douglas died on October 19, 1934 after a long illness with nephritis (Bright's disease).[10] Douglas was buried in the Nunn Cemetery in Delton, Virginia. Larry's mother stayed at the hospital in Welch, West Virginia for many hours helping to care for Douglas and many other patients who needed more attention than the hospital staff could supply. Thelma wanted to be near her son and to do all that she could to help him. The pillow Douglas used was saved and the feathers in it were wrapped together in the form of a cross. A fourth son, Doyle Bishop Rogers (Laddie) was born on June 20, 1934.

The children went everywhere with their parents. The family especially enjoyed going to visit their grandmother and grandfather Rogers' during summer vacation time. They loved to play in the shallow water by the river bank, ride in the boat, which was poled across the river to church, observe as their dad prepared his lay-lines for fishing, or sit along the river bank and watch their bamboo poles with bobbing floats and wiggle fish worms to attract the fish in the clear water. They enjoyed playing with cousins and watching for Santa to arise from behind the sofa and begin his long delivery of tons of gifts from the area of the gigantic Christmas tree at Christmas time. The parents had packed the trunk and top of the car with gifts for Santa to give the children. There were toys, clothing, pencil boxes, school supplies and other treasures from relatives. The Rogers children always celebrated Christmas at Uncle Dewey's house.

The cousins loved to gather in granddaddy's wagon, pulled by Frank and Prince, the two main farm work mules. Joe thought it was fun to run along behind the wagon where some of the kids sat with their legs dangling over the back. Joe would run with the speed of the farm wagon and lean over, face down, on the floor of the wagon, riding with legs flapping and kicking. Joe learned the hard way not to put both feet down on the ground at the same time unless he wanted to land on his nose.

Larry, Joe and Laddie were not permitted to get out of the yard at home, so they played together without many problems. They had plenty of toys and were well entertained. They went shopping, to church, or to visit friends and relatives with their parents and were content and were expected to use good manners. Mr. Rogers had a thin strip of leather about eighteen inches long to remind them of their manners when they got out of line. The boys could choose their own seats in church as long as they were closer to the pulpit than their parents and they followed their parents' rules.

There were six houses in Saw Mill Hollow, three on each side of a rut-filled road. Near the front porch of the Rogers' house was a place where Dad Rogers milked June, the family cow. The Rogers enjoyed fresh sweet milk and butter. During the depression, Everett cut hair and bartered milk and butter with customers in exchange for eggs and other things that the family needed. There was one neighbor lady who loved to talk while observing the milking process. She had a deafening laugh. She was standing near June and Mr. Rogers was milking when he skillfully focused a stream of milk into her open mouth while she was laughing. Her eyes got wide with excitement and she was eventually able to rescue her breath.

One neighbor woman had problems with some naughty neighbor kids who kept climbing into a tree in her front yard, making loud noises and awakening her sleeping baby. Her solution was unusual, but 100 percent effective. She went to the kitchen and got a pail of hot water and a long-handled dipper and cleansed the tree of its untimely visitors and restored peace to her baby's crib.

Mrs. Rogers was an excellent cook and even with a small house and close accommodations, kept many evangelists who came to their church. Rev. W. W. Carter was the most frequent houseguest. The Rogers had the opportunity to meet many great Pentecostal Holiness ministers at church revivals and at the annual Virginia Conference. The Rogers were generally elected delegates and the family looked forward to attending conference each year in Dublin, Virginia and vacationing at their grandmother's home on the New River.

Thelma Rogers baked communion bread and prepared meals for the evangelists even when they stayed elsewhere. One of the children's favorite culinary delights was when their mother would bake a gingerbread man complete with raisin eyes and buttons for their birthdays. They liked lots of cinnamon decorations and confectioner's sugar sprinkled on the gingerbread man. She was an excellent seamstress and made a lot of the shirts and other clothing that the children wore.

Off to Radford Virginia

The Rogers family decided to move back to Radford, Virginia in 1936. Mrs. Rogers had been born in Radford and had lived there until she was ten years old. The family decided to move back to the two-story frame house on a corner lot on East Second Street, where Mrs. Rogers was born in 1908. There were two old trees on the property, one furnished black heart cherries and the other, red heart cherries. Mrs. Rogers loved to make little pastry cups and fill them with delicious tart cherries with sweet whipped-cream topping. This was a special desert that the children enjoyed. While in Radford she sold Wearever Aluminum Waterless Cookware and gave demonstrations in homes.[11]

Across the street and a half block down the street was the Pentecostal Holiness Church where the Rogers attended services and Sunday school. Two of Mrs. Rogers's aunts lived in the community and the

Rogers family returned to Radford to visit them each summer. Radford was not far from the place where the Claytor Lake Dam was being built and the boys were always interested in the project. It was in this house that Mrs. Rogers lost so much of her family during the 1918 influenza epidemic.

Joe's parents decided that he should start to school in Radford. Larry was in the second grade. Joe's birthday lacked a few days of meeting the Virginia enrollment age guidelines. There were no pre-schools or kindergartens available in 1936.

Back to Six West Virginia and Saw Mill Hollow

The family decided to move back to Saw Mill Hollow in West Virginia. June, the family cow was sold, but still came to the back fence and begged to be milked. June cried and so did Mrs. Rogers when the family moved. The house in Saw Mill Hollow was still empty and school was already in session when the Rogers returned.

Mrs. Rogers agreed to teach Joe at home for a few months. Apparently, the West Virginia law regarding the beginning school age was different from the Virginia eligibility requirement. The Rogers decided to send Joe to school with his big brother Larry. Poor little Joe—still could not tie his own shoes or talk plain. He was fitted into his knickerbockers and deposited at the school along with big brother Larry. The school was so crowded that the first graders went to school for only a half-day. There was no school bus at noon to take the first graders home, so Joe was permitted to sit in the same seat with Larry in the third grade during the afternoon. The children in Larry's class were fascinated with Joe's singing and gave him marbles and sheets of notebook paper to hear him sing songs he had learned at church.

The three Rogers boys often wore homemade look-a-like clothes skillfully made by their mother and were referred to as the "green shirt boys" or something similar. Sears and Montgomery Ward mail order companies sold lots of clothing which looked alike except for the size. Hand-me-downs were popular, but by the time Larry and Joe and then Laddie grew into an outfit, it was quite worn. Mrs. Rogers insisted that the boys change into their play clothes immediately after arriving at home.

Albert McGhee was among the many preachers who stayed at the Rogers' house during revivals. He enjoyed playing with Larry's train as much as Larry did. The Rogers' household was typically relaxed and welcoming, making folks feel at home.

Caretta, West Virginia

The Carter Coal Company had tunnels all through the hills around Coalwood, Caretta and much of McDowell County.[12] Housing was available for their workers in the coal camps. They were kept in good repair and regularly maintained. The family moved to Caretta when Mr. Rogers got a job as a fire boss in the Caretta mines. Every day at 2:00 p.m. he went to work and he returned by 7:00 p.m. for supper. He walked for miles in the underground mine tunnels carrying a tool that looked like a four-foot pole with a metal point on one end during his split shift. He used this tool to tap and test the wooden beams that held up the ceiling posts at each end.

These tunnels made it possible for the low engines to pull the cars loaded with coal or miners on tracks through the mines to their work area, or to the place where the coal was washed and dumped in to huge coal cars for shipping. The mines had tipples and elevators that moved coal and miners in and out of the mines. Mr. Rogers had a light on his cap and a lantern which tested the amount of gas that was in the tunnels. Huge fans kept fresh air moving throughout the mines. Mr. Rogers worked as a fire boss until he was diagnosed with Coal Miner's Pneumoconiosis (black lung).[13]

Black lung is caused from inhaling coal dust or graphite, or man-made carbon over an extended period—a common disease among coal miners. West Virginia had a lot of soft coal mines, while hard coal mining was more popular in Pennsylvania.

There were many tragic accidents in which miners were killed. Falling kettle rock with insufficient overhead support often fell. Men sitting up too straight sometimes did not have sufficient breathing room and would inhale too much coal dust, causing them to suffocate in the flat coal cars that carried them to their work areas. Explosions caused by sudden gas buildup were a common occurrence. Canaries were sometimes taken into the mines to test the amount of gas. If there was too much gas, the birds would die. Later, special lanterns would flair a red light and sound a warning. If a person were injured, a single man was sent to inform the next of kin and if a person were killed, two men were sent with the untimely message. Such news always brought sorrow to this closely-knit community.

The depression years were difficult and people were hungry. Men often knocked on doors asking for a drink of water, a sandwich, or anything that was available to eat. Mrs. Rogers never invited a stranger into the house when her husband was away, but she brought food and water to them so they could sit on the back porch steps and eat. When Mr. Rogers was home strangers were invited to come inside and eat with the family. At one time, the Rogers permitted four men to stay in one bedroom of their four-room house since times were so difficult and they were trying to get established in a mining job.

Wash Day

Getting up early on Monday morning, Mrs. Rogers would build a fire in the cook stove and place a large galvanized tub on it which was then filled with water. The boys were expected to be on hand to carry water, get certain garments, or to perform other tasks. The boys usually worked together, but they credit Larry with being the most responsible. The Maytag washing machine was rolled into the middle of the kitchen floor and a kitchen chair was placed with on its front on the floor to supply a surface on which a tub would be placed during the washing and rinsing process. Hot water from the stove was dipped into the washing machine until it was full and the empty tub was then placed on the chair beside the washing machine and filled with cold water. A large cake of Octagon laundry soap was shaved into the Maytag to dissolve. The electric ringer extended over the tub and as clothing, starting with white items were moved around by the agitator sufficiently they were folded so the soiled water could be pressed out as the clothing passed between the rollers a second time and the clothes were ready to be hung on the clothes line to dry. Bluing was added to the rinse water to make white clothes appear brighter. All was well unless a coal engine moved empty cars around on the tracks behind the house and began to send black cinders into the air.

Following the white clothes were colored garments such as shirts, buttons folded inside and sent through the same process. White shirts were starched and/or sprinkled, rolled up and placed in the refrigerator for ironing the next day. Each wash day, all bedding was changed and all dirty clothes laundered. Mrs. Rogers kept her family clean.

Critters

At times on the way back from Six, where the Rogers attended church, they would see a stray kitten by the side of the road. Being the compassionate children that they were, they would end up taking these poor critters home, cleaning them up and keeping them for pets.

The Rogers purchased a registered Persian kitten, Topsy and he became a member of the family. The Rogers borrowed a registered Granny cat to breed with Topsy and the Rogers children had five beautiful kittens to share with friends. The children had planned to keep one of them, but ended up reclaiming another one. Boy Blue and Sambo survived nine and eleven years respectively in the Rogers' home. Topsy was later killed by the dogs when the family moved from Caretta to Yukon and Granny went back home to her previous owner.

It was at Caretta that the Rogers got their first Warm Morning® stove. A fire was easy to start if some dry wood and paper were available. It had an area where water could be poured in the back where it could evaporate and supply sufficient moisture in the air to discourage dry coughs and breathing problems. When they went to their grandparents' home for a long weekend and came back to a cold house, Mrs. Rogers would place blankets on top of the stove to warm them and then put them over the children so that they were soon toasty enough to go to sleep. They still had a cook stove that required wood or coal for cooking. It had several eyes on it where coal could be placed inside for burning. The oven baked well and it was the boys' job to scrape out the burnt coals when the stove was cold. There was a tank on one end of the stove where water could be heated for dish washing, bathing and other needs. A warming closet was located above the cooking area where delicious leftovers were saved for the next meal or for snacks later.

Piano Lessons

An evangelist came to Caretta and his song leader took an interest in the boys' singing and insisted that they should take piano lessons. The boys were scheduled for lessons and they all studied piano for two years. Joe had shown particular musical talent. Before Joe started to school, he had used one foot to pump his grandmother's pump organ and taught himself how to play the church song, "Why Not Tonight." He stood beside his mother in the Pentecostal Holiness Church choir at Six, West Virginia and sang alto with her. He had a great interest in harmony and in the second grade; the Carter Coal Company invited the Westfield's to come from New York to Caretta to organize an enriching community choir and radio program. They were quite musical and organized a radio program called The Carter Party. Joe Rogers and Violet Vipperman sang, "When I Grow Too Old to Dream" in one of the radio programs; Joe sang alto and Violet sang soprano. Both were second grade children. In music class at school, the teacher played the melody on the piano for the children to sing. Joe kept insisting that the teacher play all of it. Joe did not know that he was asking for the harmony to be played with the melody. The teacher insisted that Joe's parents should get him more involved in music.

Mrs. Nutall, the fourth grade teacher, taught the class how to play the harmonica. Each student had a book that presented songs with the syllables of words presented along with the number leading to where it could be sung or played. By each pitch there was an indication as to which hole the player should blow or draw breath through to produce the sound. It was a slow process in synchronizing the number of the hole to use and the indication to blow or draw. The teacher was surprised the next day when Joe could play all of the songs in the books by ear. *Do, mi, sol* pitches always required a blow, while all the others, *re, fa, la* and *ti* required a draw.

Joe had learned to solfeg from Rev. Jessie Barlow in a singing school at the church. [14] *Solfege* is a method used in sight-singing in which each pitch in the major scale represents a special syllable that one is to sing. Joe took piano lessons starting in the fourth grade and later earned a Master's Degree in music and taught music for forty-three years. The Rogers purchased a new piano when Joe was in the fourth grade. He quickly learned to improvise as well as to play the classics and played for himself and his brothers to sing.

New York City, Here We Come!

The Rogers family went to New York City to visit relatives and to go to the 1939 World's Fair. The three boys and their parents along with Grandmother and Granddaddy Rogers enjoyed the Fair, and visiting the Statue of Liberty, the Empire State Building and visiting Mother Roger's brother and sister. Granddaddy Rogers died shortly after returning home from the trip to New York.

Chicken Ridge

A neighbor came to the Rogers' house and mentioned that a friend from Chicken Ridge was stranded in Caretta and had no way to get back home. The Rogers agreed to take him home so both parents, three children and the stranger set out for Chicken Ridge. It was a nice Sunday drive through the mountains and they finally arrived.

The stranger insisted on giving the Rogers chickens to help show his appreciation. Mr. Rogers finally consented and they returned home with a truck filled with leg-tied chickens. It was on the way back that they heard a paper boy shouting, "Extra! Extra! Read all about it. Japan declares War!" It was December 7, 1944.

They had chicken fixed their favorite way in which Mrs. Rogers boiled it before she fried it in her delightful mixture of meal, flour, or whatever it took. The children were young and ate heartily. They had chicken salad, chicken soup, chicken sandwiches, chicken-a-la-king, chicken pot pie and even dreamed of chicken for days. They observed the hens picking up pieces of straw and throwing them over their backs, observing the signal to find a setting hen nest before she found one in a hidden place or out of reach. They later observed the little nests where baby chicks were pecking their way to freedom and located similar places to situate the hen before she laid her eggs. They soon had around a dozen baby chicks eating boiled eggs and a special formula to make them grow strong. The children were fascinated with the little jar of water turned upside down in a saucer forming a little pond from which they would get water in their mouths and hold their heads up high so they could swallow one mouth full at a time.

The chickens grew fast and when they were grown they would spread their wings to fly. Mr. Rogers clipped the feathers on one wing so they could not fly straight and flew into the side of the chicken pen. They would eat everything imaginable. Whatever they ate, the children ate second-handily and the food was delicious.

The Rogers always had fresh chicken on Sundays. At the store, the chickens' legs were tied and were placed in a paper bag with a hole for its head to hang through so it would not suffocate. At home it was placed under an upside down wash tub with a rock on top and another smaller rock under the side of the tub, lifting it just enough to get air. A container of water and some corn were added to the ensemble so that their dinner would not die during the night. On Sunday, boiling water was used to place the freshly beheaded chicken in it so the feathers would come out easily when lightly pulled. Any remaining feathers were singed or burned off when Mrs. Rogers set waded newspaper on fire in the kitchen sink. After she removed the feathers, she washed the chicken with soda and removed its stomach. After a little more cleaning the chicken was cut up and its parts boiled until tender, then rolled in a special mixture and fried to a crisp. Each member of the family had a special part they liked best. Sunday dinner was at around 3:00 and the remaining food was left on the kitchen table with a cloth over it, so that the family could return for leftovers later.

Desserts such as cake and pies were generally available along with an abundance of delicious specialties. The boys never had to make an entire meal out of something they did not like, but were required to eat a little of everything on the table. One of the Rogers' favorite snacks was cornbread and milk. A next-door neighbor looked through their window at the crusty pan of golden cornbread Mrs. Rogers had poured into a hot skillet and baked just right. He thought it was cake and made his wife prepare one for him.

Blackberries

The Rogers' boys enjoyed picking blackberries. They called the beautiful full and plump berries "lady fingers". They were delicious in a bowl of sweet milk or covered with whipped cream, or even baked in a blackberry cobbler or blackberry cake. Strawberries were another delicacy that they all enjoyed. Mrs. Rogers would make sheets of pie crust which would finish baking during dinner. The boys would hurriedly clean their plates and receive huge helpings of layer upon layer of buttered pie crust with crushed strawberries on top and between the layers.

School Lunches

It was Joe's job to prepare the sandwiches for school lunches. He would remove the outside wrapping from the lunchmeat and trim little pieces of meat and hold them up for the cats to enjoy after they had stood still in a begging position. The boys loved to take pieces of cake or pie to their school teachers and the teachers enjoyed these treats.

Yukon #2

McDowell County had some of the best schools in the coal mining area. When Larry was in Grade 9 at War Junior High School, Joe was in Grade 7. Laddie was in Grade 5 when the family moved from Caretta to Yukon #2. The children all enjoyed planting and working in the new Victory Garden, which produced plenty of tomatoes, greens and corn. A stone pig pen was located about a block from the house. Everyone looked forward to the bacon and pork chops in the fall when they passed the pigpen. Larry learned to mix the chop with the table scraps which Sally and Sara devoured in record time. Wire clamps were pressed in their snouts to discourage their attempts to move the heavy stones out of place around their pen.

Closer to the house was the chicken pen and plenty of fresh eggs. The house was somewhat larger, but they did not have an inside bathroom or inside running water. The boys missed the Caretta coal engines. The Rogers' pastor, Joe Sargent, lived just across the street. He had a stomach problem, which required that he drink goats' milk. His goats did not share his peaceful disposition; they got tired of their humble pens and kicked their way to freedom whenever they could. Brother Sargent suffered a mining injury and had to quit his job in the mines.

About three blocks away, there was a small building up on the hill where Brother Sargent preached revivals and other special services. It had a big round pot-bellied stove in the middle of the room which required kindling, charcoal, wood, coal, or whatever they could burn. There was no electricity, so Brother Sargent hung his oil lantern on a hook above the stage area so that folks could see each other, their Bibles and their hymnals. He was an excellent preacher and loved the Lord's work and put his heart into preaching; he was called on to preach revivals in surrounding areas.

During the war teachers were hard to find. Since Mrs. Rogers had teaching credentials, she was asked to teach the fifth grade at Yukon #1 Elementary School and Laddie was in her class. It was rough for him since the students were continually teasing him. Mrs. Rogers discussed this opportunity with the family before accepting the teaching position. The boys all agreed to darn their own socks, sew on buttons, and help more with the house work so that she could teach. Mrs. Rogers taught for a year or two. She learned that they needed a post mistress at Yukon #1 and she applied for the job. She got it and the family was happy.

Yukon #1

One of the Yukon #1 residents was about to lose his home, because he could not afford the mortgage payments and Mr. Rogers accepted his offer to trade houses with him. Everything worked out well. The Rogers had moved to a house within walking distance of the post office in a nice six-room house with polished hard-wood floors, inside plumbing, a Warm Morning stove and a modern kitchen. This was their home until they left for college and married.

Mrs. Rogers paid a neighbor woman to do the washing, but the boys did the rest of the housework. She said she would rather have her boys do the work than to have a stranger come to the house and do it. The boys kept the entire house clean, waxed floors, changed beds and did other household chores. Larry used the pressure cooker to prepare pinto beans on Saturdays and they learned to prepare foods for canning.

They learned how to use the electric stove in the kitchen and could prepare a cake mix, bake corn bread, chicken, or cook most any food.

Prayer and Outreach Focus

Most of us know someone in our community who is lost. Most of us will never have the opportunity to go to a foreign mission field. God has placed us in a mission field that is right where we work and live. We hear of individuals involved in drug and alcohol abuse. We hear of spouses and children who are being abused and neglected. Sin abounds in America today just as much as it did over 100 years ago when Josiah Fugate Rogers was converted. As Christians we need to become serious about praying that sinners will be converted in our communities. We need to pray for the convicting power of the Holy Spirit to stir sinners' hearts. More importantly, we need to show others the love of Christ that can change their relationships and their circumstances. The good news is that the same God who changed the lives of the Rogers family is still changing lives today.

One of Larry's aunts, Edith Barker who lived to be in her 90s, wrote a poem that captured the change in the family's religious heritage. She had several books of her poetry published. She dedicated the poem, "Lord of the Harvest" to Larry and Margaret when she wrote it in May, 1994.

Lord of the Harvest

Lord of the harvest,
your bounties never cease,
we plant and you water
and give the increase.
You send the bright sunshine
and the refreshing showers,
Lord of the harvest
and beautiful flowers.

Food for our bodies
And beauty for the eye,
Lord of the harvest,
we praise You on high.
As we work in Your harvest
may we never tire,
Lord of the harvest,
give us souls for our hire.
Bless the fruits of our labor
until the setting of the sun.
Lord of the harvest,
and our work on earth is done.

You will say to come up higher
where there is lasting joy and peace.
Where life goes on forever,
and your bounties never cease.
(Edith Barker, May 1994).[15]

28

Sarah Laurence Rogers-Larry's paternal grandmother on left.
Josiah Fugate Rogers- Larry's paternal grandfather on right.

Everett Joseph Rogers, Sr.

Everett Joseph Rogers, Sr. -Carter Coal Company Fire Boss, Caretta, West Virginia.

Thelma Bishop Rogers at Radford, Virginia home.

Thelma Bishop Rogers.

Everett Joseph Rogers, Sr. family (Back row left to right Everett, Thelma, Larry. Front row left to right Doyle (Laddie) and Joe.

Chapter Two

The Bishop Spiritual Heritage

Impress them on your children. Talk about them when you sit at home and when you walk along the road, when you lie down and when you get up (Deuteronomy 6:7).

Jesse Franklin (Frank) Bishop, Sr. and Nancy (Nannie) Flippin Bishop lived on a small farm in Patrick County, Virginia. Frank was a staunch Methodist and was a lay leader in his church. He was a government revenue officer and was paid $10.00 per moonshine still for every still that he demolished.

Nannie was a stern Primitive Baptist. She enjoyed attending her Primitive Baptist Association meetings that lasted all day with several preachers speaking and dinner on the grounds. She was a perfectionist and rarely saw humor in any situation. Frank and Nannie had four children that survived infancy. Samuel and Mattie Scott lived on a farm not far from the Bishops in Stokes County, North Carolina. Sam and Mattie attended the Asbury Methodist Church. The Scotts had ten children, five girls and five boys. They were all hard working and moved from one tenant farm to another to improve their crop yield.

Reverend Jordan from Georgia conducted a revival in the Asbury community and the Bishop and Scott families attended the services. Most people walked to the services or rode horseback. Some walked for miles to the building they called Antioch, because they were so hungry to hear the Word of God. The Holy Spirit convicted sinners and lives were changed and renewed in these services. Revivals often lasted for weeks. This particular revival with Rev. Jordan had a legendary impact on the Asbury community. The love of God reigned in the hearts of the seekers that attended these meetings. Neighbors and family members that had once been enemies had been changed by the power of the Holy Spirit and could now love one another.

They decided to form a new church and were influenced by Rev. Jordan who was a preacher in the newly formed Pentecostal Holiness Church to become a part of that denomination. The group did not have a permanent structure for a church until several years later when they formed the Mountain View Pentecostal Holiness Church in what was then called Brim, Virginia and later renamed Claudville, Virginia.

Frank and Nannie Bishop both joined the new Pentecostal Holiness Church. This decision to join the same church brought a new sense of unity to their home. Nannie told of an experience that she had when she was praying and began to speak in a strange language. She humbly asked the Lord to help her to know what she was saying. The Lord gave her the interpretation of this message. This was a special memory for her and an experience that many others had during this time of intensely seeking God.

Jesse Franklin Bishop, Jr. and Mabel Scott became acquainted during the revival and continued to attend the newly formed Pentecostal Holiness Church with their parents. They talked about the young people walking for miles together in large groups to church. Many of these young people developed relationships that were to last a lifetime. Jesse quickly claimed Mabel as his sweetheart. Jesse Franklin Bishop, Jr. and Mabel Marie Scott were married on December 19, 1932 in Stokes County, North Carolina. Like many young couples during that period, they moved in with Jesse's parents until they could afford to rent their first home. Jesse started a tobacco crop to support his young bride.

Margaret Estelle Bishop

Jesse loved to tell stories. His favorite stories revolved around his five children. Jesse and Mabel's first child, Margaret Estelle Bishop was born on September 30, 1933. Jesse gave the doctor a ham for delivering Margaret. Little Margaret soon won Nannie Bishop's heart. She brought a smile to her face and a laugh that no one else could bring.

Mabel told that she and Jesse first took Margaret to church with them when she was a week old. She wailed so loudly that Mabel had to take her outside. Afterwards, she told Jesse that she was not going to take that child to church again until she was grown. They later learned that the baby was having trouble digesting milk. They did not know what the problem was for some time. One day Jesse and Mabel laid little Margaret on the bed and Jesse prayed, "Lord, you have given us this child and she is yours to take back. Otherwise you can heal her."[1] The next week the doctor suggested that perhaps the cow's milk may have been contaminated and offered to trade cows with them. Little Margaret was fine and began to grow and became a healthy child after that.

The family enjoyed visiting with Sam and Mattie Scott, Mabel's parents. Grandma Scott allowed Margaret to sit at the first table with the adults while the younger ones had to wait. Her younger siblings soon nick named her, "Grandma's little angel." According to them, Margaret could do no wrong around Grandma Scott.

First houses

Jesse and Mabel soon moved to a two-room house over the hill from Jesse's parents. Aileen was born on January 23, 1935. Grandma Bishop and Iowa Anderson were with Mabel waiting for the midwife before Aileen was born. Iowa remembers when Aileen was born that Margaret toddled over to the dresser drawer that held the baby clothes and brought clothes for the baby. Jesse told that he gave the midwife a dough tray that he had made for delivering Aileen. Marie was born on April 15, 1936. No one remembers what Jesse bartered for her delivery.

Later they moved to Stokes County, North Carolina and Jesse and Mabel shared a large two-story farm house with Frank and Ima Scott. Frank was Mabel's brother and Ima was Jesse's sister. The Bishops lived in one end of the house and the Scotts lived on the other end with their daughter, Vernice. They called this house the Josh house. The two young families shared together in all of the joys and sorrows and hard work, as well as fun times. Laughter and singing were familiar sounds around the Bishop and Scott households. Vernice became like another sister to the Bishop girls.

Mabel wrote about the early days of their marriage:

We were happily married though very poor. One of my greatest ambitions was to live a Christian life. I wanted to be a good wife and if we had children to teach them to love and serve God. I remember the first meal that I prepared. We had moved in our first little humble home. We sat down and I looked at Jesse and said, "You say the blessing." He said, "You go ahead." I said, "You are the head of the house." After that, Jesse always said the blessing. We began a family altar in our home and tried to build our home on a foundation of faith[2] (Mable Bishop's unpublished journal).

Jesse and Mabel always began and ended the day with prayer. Their little giggly girls had to have a lot of instruction about being reverent during prayer time. Jesse knew that the girls all liked for him to rub their heads and so, he would tell them that if they would not misbehave during prayer time that he would rub their heads. This became a special time and the girls were always disheartened if they had misbehaved and did not get their heads rubbed. One time Vernice came over and Jesse invited her to pray with the family. She was excited to be with her cousins and she could not contain herself. She talked and giggled. After Jesse finished praying, he rubbed all of the Bishop girl's heads, but did not rub Vernice's head. Vernice went back to her mother crying and screaming. Her mother wanted to know what was wrong. "Uncle Jesse wouldn't rub my head," she wailed.

Aunt Ima soothingly said, "Come here and I'll rub your head."

"No, it won't be the same," Vernice insisted. She had learned an important lesson that day.

Uncle Frank got a trucking job in Virginia. This meant that Jesse's family needed a smaller place with land that they could farm. Jesse and Mabel moved their family to a small log cabin in Westfield, North Carolina on Jesse's cousin's farm in Asbury, North Carolina shortly before Yvonne was born. The log house had a kitchen and one big room on the first floor and a large bedroom on the second floor. Jesse constructed a heater out of a large metal barrel. He sawed the wood to fit this heater. The girls soon discovered that the logs made a perfect stool. Each evening at prayer time, each child took a log and seated herself next to the warm heater. Jesse would read from the Bible and sometimes Mabel would read from a Bible story book. The children were expected to be reverent during the family devotion time. One time, Jesse was reading from Psalm 108:9 about Moab being a wash pot. Marie found this verse amusing as she imagined Moab being like the huge wash pot that she had seen her mother use to wash their clothes. Marie toppled off of her stool laughing, "Moab, is my wash pot." Mabel and the other girls started laughing and even Jesse had to admit that this was funny.

The girls all stayed in the upstairs bedroom. The exposed rafter overhead was a hiding place where the parents hid Christmas toys. The little girl's eyes soon discovered the hiding place and began climbing up and getting into gifts and playing with them secretly before Christmas.

Yvonne was born on November 25, 1938. Jesse's sister, Ima assisted Mabel when Yvonne was born. Jesse and Uncle Frank had gone to get the doctor in Jesse's Model-A Ford. The doctor stopped by the fireplace to warm his hands when he came in the house. Aunt Ima and Mabel had decided to play a practical joke on the doctor and hid Yvonne under the covers. While the doctor was warming his hands and chatting with Jesse by the fire, Yvonne wailed out big and loud. The doctor abruptly turned and said, "That baby has already been born!" They all got a big laugh. Jesse gave the doctor two squirrels that he had shot that morning and sent him on his way. The next morning the older sisters were taken to see their baby sister. They all politely admired the tiny baby except for two-year-old Marie who looked at her mother and disapprovingly blurted out, "Why did you have to go and get an old baby?"

Margaret Murdered Yvonne

When Yvonne was a baby, Margaret and her other sisters all wanted to take turns holding and playing with the new baby. Mabel firmly admonished them to be careful when they held her and told them that if they dropped her they would kill her. One day, Mabel went out to hang clothes and Margaret and the other girls were playing with the baby near the tub where their mother had been washing clothes. Margaret slipped in the water near the wash tub and dropped the baby. Margaret and the other girls went running outside and Mabel asked them what they had done with Yvonne. "We killed Yvonne!" Margaret sobbed. Mabel went frantically running in the house to find little Yvonne on the floor squalling where she had been dropped. The sisters had taken their mother literally when she told them that they would kill the baby if they dropped her and had assumed that since they had dropped her that she must be dead.

Bath Time

Jesse and Mabel had an assembly line arrangement when bath time came. Jesse brought in the galvanized wash tub, filled it with hot water from the stove and cooled it with spring water. Mabel stripped the first one down and Jesse bathed that child as she stripped the second one. He dried, powdered, and handed one back to her mother to put clean clothes on until all four were scrubbed and clean. They were placed in the other room to wait for their parents to bathe and dress. When all were ready, they would pile in the old Model-A Ford.

The old Ford sputtered along the old country road to church, stopping to pick up walkers to ride the running boards. Jesse and Mabel continued to be involved in church and attended regularly. Mabel was elected to be the church secretary.

The Model A Gets Led Astray

Yvonne liked to play in the old Model A. Margaret and her other sisters would try to keep her away from the car. One day she sneaked out and got up in the car and knocked it out of gear. Her dad was in the front yard and saw the car backing out of the drive way. He ran and caught up with it, stood on the running board and steered it until it stopped. Yvonne came up the steps of the back porch where Margaret had gone to the well to draw water. She was only three years old and was too excited to tell how she got out of the car. Her guardian angel was definitely on board!

The Asbury Pentecostal Holiness Church

Lossie Flippin, Nannie Bishop's brother owned several farms in the Asbury community. He heard that a large school building adjoining one of his farms was for sale because the school had been consolidated with the school in Francisco. Lossie purchased the school and gave it to the newly formed Pentecostal Holiness Church to hold their worship services. The church soon got a pastor, Reverend James Hutchins.

Most of the families had lots of children and they soon recognized the need to start a Sunday school to train the children. The children were all expected to learn the books of the Bible and memory verses each week. They would have the children to come up every Sunday and recite the memory verses that they had learned and to sing. Every summer, a camp meeting was held in a large tent on the grounds and people came from distant cities and camped out in tents and campers to hear invited speakers and singers. The meetings usually lasted for about ten days.

The farms in the area were all tobacco farms. The Pentecostal Holiness Church strongly stood against the manufacture and use of tobacco products from its inception even before tobacco was considered a health hazard. The men were not permitted to serve as deacons in the local church because they were tobacco farmers. The women served as deaconesses since there were no men to serve.

The Family Outlaw

Jesse James Bishop was born on September 13, 1943 in Stokes County, North Carolina. Jesse and Mabel's pastor, James Hutchins had come to visit before the delivery of their fifth child. Jesse was so thrilled to finally have a son after four daughters that he grabbed Jimmy Hutchins. The two of them danced a jig in the middle of the living room floor and Jesse said, "I'm going to name him after me and you." Mabel immediately protested about her son's name because she did not want him to share the name of the famous outlaw. She would call him, "Little Jimmy." Yvonne liked to correct her when company came to visit and say, "But his real name is Jesse James." Jesse gave the doctor $5.00 for delivering Jim.

The next morning, Jesse called up the stairs and said, "Girls come down and see what we have!" They all bounded down the stairs as proud Jesse pulled the cover back from Jim's face to show them the new baby. Marie said that she wanted to see his feet. Jesse told her that it was too cold to uncover his feet.

Marie retorted, "Well, I'm not going to school until I see his feet." Mabel slowly uncovered the baby's feet to show Marie. The girls all then skipped off to school singing, "We have a little brother."

Family Times

All of the children were made to feel like they were the only child on many occasions. Despite their poverty stricken means, their parents always tried to do things that were special for each of them and to spend time with them individually. Mable knew certain foods that were favorites with each of them and would try to incorporate these into her menus. She would take fabric scraps from a dress that she had made one of them and make a dress for a doll and would crochet things for them.

Tobacco curing season was a favorite time for all of the children. Jesse harvested the tobacco leaves and brought a load at a time on a slide pulled by the mule to the barn. Mabel would tie the tobacco leaves together and loop them with string around a long pole. The girls made an assembly line each handing three leaves at a time to her until the pole was full. Then she would hang it in the barn to cure. Jesse would keep a fire going in the furnace all night long to facilitate the curing process. The fire had to be kept at a consistent temperature. The Bishop family would gather under the shelter at the barn and have family prayer. Then Mabel would take all of the children except one back to put them to bed. One child was allowed to stay with Jesse each night to help tend the fire. This was a special treat, because he would always take some apples to roast over the fire and would tell some of his favorite tales while the apples roasted. They all still fondly remember the tobacco barn apples and the stories.

Jesse used this individual time with his children to teach them about his faith. He would always say, "Now count the stars and see how many you can count before you go to sleep."[3] He would remind them that God had told Abraham that his descendants would be as many as the stars in the sky and that He could call each star by name. Jesse Bishop was proud of his children. He felt blessed with each new addition to the family like the psalmist who said, "Blessed is the man who hath his quiver full of them" (Psalm 127:5). He had a jolly sense of humor and yet knew how to command authority in his household.

All of the children remember as a part of their early training that time was set aside each evening for Bible reading, reciting scriptures and prayers. Jesse would announce after supper, "Come over here and sit down while I read the Bible." He would read and then pick a verse and ask each of the children to recite it or question them about a part of the text which he had read. Sometimes, he would quiz them through the day with questions like, "What were Isaiah's two son's names?"

Jesse wanted the girls to sing in church beginning at an early age. Before they were tall enough to see over the pulpit, he would stand them up on top of it and tell them to sing. Uncle Frank bought a recorder to record the family singing. He would play a harmonica and the family would sing. Jesse would write poetry and recite it on the records.

Playing School, Church & Wedding

The Bishop girls enjoyed playing school as children. It was always understood that Margaret was the teacher and the younger girls were her pupils. They also liked to play church. Margaret was always the preacher. When the children would play church, they sometimes mimicked local church members and preachers.

The children in the area often heard their parents and neighbors in the woods behind their homes praying for lost souls and sometimes even the children would turn play time into sincere prayer meetings. Most of them did not actually commit their lives to Christ until they were older.

Blackberry Dresses

A lady in Claudeville, Virginia offered the girls their first job picking blackberries for a few cents a gallon. After she would pay them for the berries, their mother would take them to Mount Airy and they would pick out cotton prints to make dresses. When she would make the dresses they would call them their blackberry dresses. Several years later they learned that the lady that hired them was having them pick berries for her winery.

Margaret's Early Years

Margaret began school at Francisco Elementary School in Francisco, North Carolina. Soon Aileen and Marie were school age and joined her for the daily walk to catch the school bus. They also had cousins at that school. The girls were enrolled in Red Bank Elementary School for two years when they moved to Claudeville, Virginia.

Jesse Moves to West Virginia

There was a great demand for coal to fire the steal furnaces during the war to manufacture planes and weapons. Jesse's brother, Barzy and his wife, Essie and sons Herman, Vernon and Tom moved to Caretta, West Virginia. Barzy got a job in the mines as a blacksmith. Shortly after Jim was born, Jesse gave up tobacco farming and got a job at the coal mines and moved to Caretta, West Virginia to stay with Barzy and his family. Jesse worked as an aerial tram operator, lifting the buckets of coal slack out of the mines and sending them to the slate dump on the mountain.

There had been such a huge influx of miners during this time that there was not sufficient housing. Jesse moved his family into Uncle Frank's house in Claudeville, Virginia until he could find a house in West Virginia for the family. Mabel did not have a car while Jesse was away so she and the girls would walk everywhere and carry baby Jim. They would walk to church for two services on Sunday and to prayer meeting on Wednesday nights. Mabel would gather the children around for prayer time each morning and evening. She taught the children that they needed to depend on the Lord during this critical time in their family when their father was away.

The war years were difficult. It was two years before Jesse could find a house in West Virginia and the family could all be together again. Jesse would come home every other weekend to be with his family. The Carter Coal Company eventually built company houses for the miners to rent. Jesse and Mabel moved their family to Caretta near Barzy's family in 1944. The children were delighted at the prospect of moving to their new home in West Virginia to be with their dad. It was a difficult time for Mabel to leave all of her family and friends in Virginia and North Carolina and the church to move to West Virginia.

The little four room company house where they moved with the white picket fence was always immaculate. All of the company-owned houses on the street looked alike and were all painted routinely with gray paint. The Bishops took pride in their new abode. The girls remember sweeping the whole yard and their mother kept the inside spotless. She would say, "Let's keep things looking nice, because someone might come." The neighbors were close and someone was always stopping by to visit.

The girls enjoyed their new school and meeting friends in West Virginia. However, attending church in West Virginia was not quite so pleasant. Rev. Joe Sargent had gotten to know Jesse at the mines and had invited him to come to help him in the new church at Yukon #2. There were no other young people at his church and the children often complained about having to go to church where there were no young people. The culture was different. They had been surrounded by cousins and people with similar values in Claudeville. They did not understand why they had to go to church. They remember how that on numerous occasions, Jesse would sit them down and tell them that God wanted them to be a blessing to these people that had just come to know the Lord.

The girls had leadership opportunities in this small church that they probably would not have had at a larger church. They taught Sunday school classes and led in other areas of youth ministries. They were all involved with the music.

Revival broke out after the young pastor, T. L. Lowery and his wife, Mildred, came and many new young people began to come. There was a mighty move of the Holy Spirit working among the youth as well as the adults. They started a 15-minute radio broadcast on Sunday mornings in Welch. It was about a 40-minute ride across the mountains to the radio station before church. Margaret and Marie were invited to go along and sing the opening and closing song for the program. The church bought a bus that would pick up people to attend all church meetings. This meant that the Bishop girls could go to church when their father had to work.

Jesse began to prepare to become an ordained minister in the Pentecostal Holiness Church. He pastored several Pentecostal Holiness churches in West Virginia including Premier, Coalwood, Six and War. He built the church in Coalwood, West Virginia, while working full time and going to visit Mabel each week in the sanitarium in Beckley. The coal miners and their families were faced with many hardships and uncertainties. There were layoffs, strikes and the mining accidents which claimed many lives.[4]

It was only their faith and reliance upon God that sustained them through these times. Throughout these years the Bishop children saw the consistency with which their parents lived their Christian lives. The family prayer, Bible reading and church attendance continued whether there were strikes, illnesses, disappointments or hardships.

Margaret wrote that "If one of the children needed shoes, they learned to ask the Lord and to trust Him to supply the need. Those lessons of faith followed us into our adult years. We learned that God never fails. Jesus's promise was to be with us always even to the end of the age. What a legacy!" (Sketches of our Bishop heritage-unpublished document).[5]

The Bishop children were always taught to have compassion on those in their community and around the world who were less fortunate. They were taught to help those in need. They can remember their mother making a dress for someone or taking food to a family in need.

The coal mining community provided a multicultural experience for the young Bishop children. Immigrants from many different countries migrated to West Virginia to seek their fortune in the coal mines. There were Hungarian, Polish, Irish, Italian and many other nationalities in the neighborhood where the Bishops lived. This small yet cosmopolitan community prepared Margaret for the many different people groups that she would later interact with in Morocco and Marie for her work in Kenya.

Prayer and Outreach Focus

There are many missions' opportunities in your own community that involve witnessing and working with people that you would not encounter in church. Prisoners need to hear the gospel of Jesus Christ. There are people in the hospitals some of whom are at Death's door who need to hear the Gospel and do not have a church or a pastor. There are people in rehabilitation centers who desperately want to turn their lives around and need to be told that they can have hope in Jesus Christ. There are elderly folks in nursing homes that are lonely and need to hear about the love and comfort of the scriptures. There are people who have lost their jobs, their homes and everything they own. Your church can reach out to these people and show them the love of Christ during their difficult circumstances.

Jesse Franklin Bishop, Sr. and Nancy Bishop, Myrtle (standing)
and baby, Jesse Franklin Bishop, Jr.

Jesse Franklin Bishop, Jr.

Mabel Bishop.

Jesse Franklin Bishop, Jr. and Mabel Bishop (top row)
Margaret, Aileen, Marie (middle row), Yvonne and Jim (lower row).

Chapter Three

Conversation Stories

Train a child in the way he should go, and when he is old
he will not depart from it (Proverbs 22:6).

Margaret's Conversion

The Bishop girls had a healthy family sibling rivalry from an early age. Marie tells about asking her mother to take the broom to bed with her in case Margaret tried to pick a fight with her. Aileen wrote that Margaret was born into a leadership role as the oldest of five children. Margaret valued her prayer time early in life. Aileen and the other girls remember her getting up early in the morning to build a fire in the old coal kitchen range and kneeling to pray before the others got up for school.

Margaret's Conversion Story

Margaret tells the story of her conversion:

"During the early years growing up on the farm in western North Carolina, we youngsters enjoyed playing in the surrounding woods and playhouses. We often had prayer meetings in the wooded areas as we had seen the adults from the church do on many occasions. Sometimes these were spiritual, but it took several years to bring maturity and understanding of what becoming a Christian might entail. During the preteen years, I observed in meetings at the church when altar calls were given that this part of the service was serious. Conviction of right and wrong became very evident and I knew that I needed to choose the right. Conviction was so strong that I could feel the devil chasing me, enticing me to do what was wrong. Such an unhappy feeling resulted that I wanted to get rid of the devil following me. In my childish mind I thought that perhaps if I hurried to the door, slamming it quickly behind me, I could get him off my case. It did not take long to realize that he was not going to leave me alone.

After moving to southern West Virginia while I was in the sixth grade, community church across from the school was having a children's crusade after school. They invited children to stop in on their way from school and to bring their parents with them. Mother joined me as I went to the service. As the minister was giving his sermon, he noted my interest and saw the conviction on my face. He came up to me and asked if I would like to come up to pray. In my preteen mind, I saw him as a Methodist minister and I did not want to get saved in a Methodist church, so I shook my head "no." After we came home, Mother asked me about it and I told her that I did not want to pray with the minister. She let the matter rest and I am sure that she pondered it often in prayer.

The following summer we were in the western North Carolina area for vacation. The Asbury Pentecostal Holiness Church was having a camp meeting and we attended the services. On the first night as the altar call was given, I felt terribly convicted and my first cousin, Virginia, came to me and reached out her hand. She didn't even have to say a word and I followed her to the altar where she prayed with me and I gave my heart to the Lord. What a wonderful relief to be free of that conviction and to be right with the Lord! This was a blissful time and I soon took on new responsibilities as our family returned to our church in West Virginia and I told the pastor about my conversion. On Sunday morning he called on me to lead the prayer to open Sunday school. I froze in my tracks, but bravely ventured a try. From this I learned that each time I tried I became stronger. The growing process had begun."

Marie tells about the difference in the Bishop household after Margaret was converted. She remembers coming home from school and hearing Margaret praying. Marie talked about a peace that would come over all of them when Margaret prayed for them. Margaret and Marie were baptized in the Dan River one summer when they went to Claudeville, Virginia to visit relatives. Aileen wrote that parents of teens always felt at ease to have their teen in a group that included Margaret. They knew Margaret was a good Christian role model for their teens.

Margaret felt that God was calling her to Christian service at age 16. One summer day Margaret and her sisters and some cousins were talking about going to the lake. They decided to have a prayer meeting instead. The girls were playing the piano and singing and had decided that perhaps Margaret's idea to have a prayer meeting was not so bad. Margaret tells about the spirit falling during that prayer meeting and it was at that time that she felt a call to Christian service. Her sister Aileen remembers this prayer meeting and says that no one in the room could have doubted that Margaret was called to Christian service after this event.

Margaret immediately began to become involved in ministry opportunities. She taught Sunday school classes and helped with vacation Bible school in her dad's churches. She got her mission worker's license in 1955.

Larry's Conversion Story

Larry became a Christian when he was eleven years old. Larry's brothers remember that he was deeply committed to following Christ and to His service. Joe commented that "when Larry got home from school, he went to his room, threw the covers over his head and spent time in prayer, crying out to God." They were all involved in the church and took the work of the Lord seriously.

Larry's dedication, motivation, desire and love for God were obvious throughout his life. He consistently sought the Lord for opportunities to serve others and to spread the Gospel of Jesus Christ.

Prayer and Outreach Focus

Larry and Margaret were both converted as children. Childhood evangelism is a wide open field in any community. There are children in your church that are just waiting for someone to take the time with them to lead them to Christ. There are children in your schools and neighborhoods who may have never had the opportunity to come to church and hear the Gospel. Be open to opportunities that may be available in your area to share the Gospel with children. We can save them so much pain if we can lead them to Christ as children and they will not have to endure the scars of sin as adolescents and adults.

Chapter Four

Margaret's College Days

Trust in the Lord in all your ways and lean not to your own understanding (Proverbs 3:5).

Margaret wanted to attend a Bible college after she graduated from high school. She began to pray about an opportunity to continue her education. A neighbor minister's wife, Lilia Wood, showed Margaret a college annual from Holmes Bible College in Greenville, South Carolina where she and her husband had attended.[1] Margaret sent an application and prayed that she would be accepted. She received a letter a few weeks later stating that the college had reached its enrollment capacity for the coming year and encouraged her to reapply the following year.

The summer after Margaret graduated from high school she went to work in a hosiery mill in Mt. Airy, North Carolina. As Margaret left home, her mother admonished her to not let her work or her new associates cause her to become slack in her prayer life. Margaret tried to follow her mother's advice and the Holy Spirit caused her to become hungrier for God. One Sunday evening while she was with a group of young people, she suggested that they have a prayer meeting. They all prayed and during that meeting, Margaret felt the Holy Spirit calling her to preach the Gospel to the lost. She wrote, "I knew that as a result of my calling a transition would soon come. My job was no longer interesting to me, for I felt that I did not fit in with this mindset of earning money merely to satisfy my earthly desires"[2] (Pentecostal Holiness Advocate, February 2, 1956).

In early October, Margaret received another letter from Holmes College of the Bible informing her that someone had dropped out and that she could now enroll if she wished to do so. Margaret thought that she would continue to work another year before leaving. Her Aunt Ima encouraged her to go ahead and go. Her Aunt Ima reasoned that if she waited she may decide not to go the following year.

Uncle Frank drove Margaret to the bus station in Mt. Airy, North Carolina where she took the bus to Greenville, South Carolina in the fall of 1952 to begin her preparation for Christian service at Holmes College of the Bible. She told about the other students meeting her at the bus station welcoming her to college life. She knew that she had done the right thing to listen to her Aunt Ima and to start her studies immediately. While Margaret was a student at Holmes College of the Bible, several students related their experiences with being called to foreign fields to her. She admired their willingness to sacrifice for God in such a way and she was grateful for the opportunity to associate with such consecrated people.

During Margaret's second year at Holmes College of the Bible, Margaret began to feel a definite call on her life to become a missionary. She quickly realized the weighty responsibilities that would follow if she were to respond to this call. The Lord gave her the scripture Psalms 50:12-15 that would serve as both a challenge and a source of strength as she continued to prepare to respond to this call:

If I were hungry I would not tell thee; for the world is mine and the fullness thereof. Offer unto God thanksgiving and pay thy vows unto the Most High. And call upon me in the day of trouble; and I will deliver thee and thou shalt glorify me.

Her roommates were Fannie Lowe and Coreen Caudele. Fannie Lowe was to become a long time missionary to China. Margaret told about giving Fannie Lowe her nick name while they were in college. Fannie and Margaret were talking one day about names. Fannette Lowe confessed that she did not like her name. Margaret said, "Well, we could just call you 'Fannie.'" The name stuck and most people only knew her by her nickname after that.

Margaret served in the school cafeteria where she cooked biscuits at 5:00 a.m. each morning. She also worked in the college library located in the Holmes Memorial Building. She tells about a young man named Elvio Canavasio coming to the library. Elvio had recently come to America and had very limited English. He was determined to become proficient in the English language and would often ask Margaret to explain a passage that he was reading. If he did not understand her explanation, he would ask, "What do you mean?" She would continue to attempt to explain until he understood. She worked for Miss Della Wade cleaning her house while she was a student where she earned extra money to pay her laundry bill. There were no laundry facilities in the dorm and students had to send their laundry to a local laundry facility each week. At the end of Margaret's first year, she scored a 95 on her Bible exam.

Margaret returned home to help with vacation Bible school and to visit with her mother in the sanitarium during the summer after her second year at Holmes. It was during this summer that she met a young man named Larry Rogers at a cottage prayer meeting at Uncle Barzy and Aunt Essie's house. Larry had started a vacation Bible school program at the War Pentecostal Holiness Church. He asked Margaret to travel with him to different churches to train other teachers. She would share a mission story with the children each evening. Aileen, Marie and Yvonne taught classes in the vacation Bible schools. Aileen had a summer job in North Carolina.

Margaret completed her final year as salutatorian of her class. She graduated from Holmes College of the Bible in 1955. Margaret's parents were not able to attend her graduation because her mother was in the sanitarium. Marie and her husband had a 1951 Studebaker. Marie and Aileen decided to make the trip from West Virginia to Greenville, South Carolina in the Studebaker. When they got to Mt. Airy, North Carolina the car started stalling every time they would stop at a stoplight. They would have to get someone to push the car every time they started. Finally a nice man in a bread truck noticed their plight and pushed them though every stoplight from Mt. Airy to Gastonia, North Carolina.

They had never been in a city with the stoplights on the side of the street before they got to Greenville, South Carolina. When they got to Greenville, they noticed that cars were screeching on the brakes every time they would go through an intersection. They ran through several red lights before they observed that the stoplights were located on the side of the street instead of dangling overhead in the middle of the street. The girls made it safely to Margaret's graduation thanks to many guardian angels.

They were proud to attend this event for their older sister and to hear her deliver her salutatorian address. After Margaret graduated, Dr. Paul F. Beacham asked her to remain on campus to teach. She expressed her gratitude for his offer, but insisted that she must return home to West Virginia to help her family while her mother was in the sanitarium.

Larry's College Days

Reverend C. R. and Martha Woodard at the War Pentecostal Holiness Church and numerous other capable ministers and missionaries of the Virginia Conference of the Pentecostal Holiness Church served as mentors for Larry in his early ministry.

Larry graduated from Big Creek High School in 1948.[3] He had not told his family about his call to the ministry until his senior year in high school. One day his mother was trying to ascertain his plans so that the family could plan and budget accordingly. Larry finally burst into tears and announced that he had been called to the ministry. Joe remembers that they were all caught off guard at this announcement, but were not surprised because of his dedication.

Larry's parents along with Joe and Laddie drove Larry to Emmanuel College in the fall of 1948.[4] After they had unloaded Larry's belongings, they started the trip home late at night under a cold, dark, moonless night sky. Larry's brothers remember that the trip was fairly uneventful until Mother Nature called. There were no service stations or anywhere to stop within miles during these late night and early morning hours. Finally, Mr. Rogers stopped beside the high way on a narrow mountain road, turned off the car lights and waited as the boys relieved themselves. They assumed that both boys had gotten back in the car when they heard the door shut and started on their way. They heard Joe giggling in the back seat and were surprised when he told them that they had left Laddie. Mr. Rogers stopped and heard Laddie clomping down the road as fast as he could go trying to catch up with the car.

While Larry was at Emmanuel College he was involved in several extracurricular activities. He served as vice president of the sophomore class, treasurer of the Boys Evangelistic Club, was a member of the Save-A-Soul Club and sang in a mixed choral group and in an octet.

Larry enjoyed a revival at Emmanuel College which the students at that time will never forget. He remembered that he and June Carter Canavesio were hardly able to speak in English for some time after the revival. They were continuously speaking in other languages as the Holy Spirit moved in their lives and across the campus. The entire campus was experiencing a great revival. Even in the classrooms the professors allowed the students to spend time in prayer. Larry appreciated the dear friends that he met at Emmanuel College and continued to correspond with many of them.

He spoke of how Jack Carter while praying for the healing of a friend, was marvelously healed himself. Jack Carter had been stricken with polio while he was driving in Canada. He had let the car drift to a stop to let his dad drive because he had insufficient control of his limbs. While he was praying at Emmanuel College, he began to feel rejuvenating nerve sensation in his limbs and rejoiced that he had been healed while praying for his friend.

Larry mentioned inspiring friends such a James Newton, Norman Ford, and Durant Driggers to name only a few who became friends for life. Larry left Emmanuel College a different person. He was determined to fulfill his call as a missionary for the Lord. James Newton remembers that Larry was quite a prayer warrior and a good preacher. James and Larry preached revivals together in several West Virginia churches after graduating from Emmanuel College. They also conducted several vacation Bible schools.

James enrolled at Holmes Theological Seminary after he graduated from Emmanuel College. He was asked to teach at Holmes Theological Seminary after graduating. James married Adeline Law from Millboro, Virginia and remained at Holmes Theological Seminary with his family until his retirement in 2011. James Newton remembers teaching Margaret at Holmes Theological Seminary when she was a student and he was a student teacher. He remembers her being a dedicated young lady.

Larry became a leader in daily vacation Bible schools after his first year at Emmanuel College. He worked in the Bible schools and with revivals at Yukon #1, Six, War and anywhere he had the opportunity to serve the Lord. He was devoted and spent much time in prayer, crying out to God for the souls that were to be touched in the vacation Bible schools. His brothers helped him, Joe playing the piano and Laddie leading the singing.

Larry graduated from Emmanuel College in 1950 and enrolled at Concord College near Princeton, West Virginia. He found the dorm life at Concord totally unappealing. He told his parents about the beer bottles being rolled down the halls and about the cheating and corrupt attitudes and activities that were part of college life. His mother was still in contact with some of the childhood friends that she had met at the Odd Fellows Home and one of her acquaintances, 'Lefty' Johnson, was an administrator at Bob Jones University in Greenville, South Carolina. Mr. Johnson encouraged her to send Larry to Bob Jones University and so in the middle of a school year, Larry transferred to Bob Jones University.

Larry loved the dorm life at Bob Jones University with other fine Christian young men and together they soaked up the inspiring chapel messages by Dr. Bob Jones, Sr., Dr. Bob Jones, Jr., and many other great Christian giants who spoke such as Dr. Oswald J. Smith and Dr. James McGinley. He enjoyed the instruction in the preacher boy class with instructors such as Dr. Frances Shaeffer, Dr. Stenholm and numerous other successful pastors, evangelists and missionaries.

Each dorm room had accommodations for five students with bunk beds and a large desk made to accommodate two students located by a huge window. Air conditioning was not available during those days and at times during the day, it was quite hot. Most nights were cool and comfortable. The library was a favorite place for studying as were the large classroom buildings where campus students could study in groups or alone, since there were no night classes. Larry honored the university rules requiring punctuality for work assignments and classes. Griping was not tolerated, boys and girls did not touch each other, and students got demerits for infractions. The radio station was named WMUU for Worlds' Most Unusual University.

During Larry's second year at Bob Jones University, Joe joined him and they were able to room together. Both boys waited tables in the college dining room for $.33 per hour to help with expenses which were $800.00 per year for each student. There were eight students sitting at each table, the host at one end, hostess at the other end and three students on each side. Someone would make the announcements and recognize guests and then ask the blessing. The 'Amen' signaled the waiters to leave the kitchen and to proceed down the aisles to their individual tables where they had prepared each place setting in advance. Food was handed to the hostess at each table who passed each container to her right and it continued around the table family style. When everyone had been served, the hostess placed her fork on her plate and everyone was free to begin eating. If one bowl did not have enough servings for eight people, the hostess informed the waiter and he brought another bowl. When all had finished the main courses, the waiters brought the dessert.

Larry and Joe were both anxious to become involved in actual ministry and found that waiting tables limited their filling pulpits and accepting invitations to sing or play for church groups. During Larry's senior year and Joe's sophomore year, they went out on Fridays and worked with the New Life Mission on Biltmore Avenue in Asheville, North Carolina and held Bible schools on Saturdays. Larry cooked pots of beans, made cakes, cleaned, instructed, preached, passed out tracts and welcomed men who passed by the store-front chapel, or did whatever was needed. The boys preached, gave their testimonies, sang with the men, played musical instruments, prayed with individuals, encouraged, or knelt beside them, opened their Bibles, pointed out salvation scriptures and read them aloud. They rejoiced as men prayed the sinner's prayer and were sometimes recipients of a bear hug from a crying man realizing the joy of sins forgiven and experiencing his position as a new creation in Christ.

During Joe's second year, both boys stayed in an eight-foot-wide trailer in a nearby trailer court to help cut expenses. They put newspapers between the bed covers to help keep out the cold that winter. They were glad when spring arrived. Another year while other students continued the Biltmore mission project, Larry opened up a mission in an intersection called Five Points in Asheville, North Carolina. Larry's heart was heavy for the men in that area and the work was very difficult to manage as a full time university student. His challenge of taking Greek and Hebrew at the same time with the rest of his classes became a tremendous burden. Larry talked about Mrs. Genetti, the mother of the late Phillip Genetti, Sr. being a supporter at the mission and how that her prayers were instrumental in a wealth of souls being brought in the kingdom through the Five Points Mission.

Larry, no doubt, in heaven will be greeted by a huge crowd of Asheville citizens who walked briskly through the back alleys and streets of Asheville during their childhood years, following Larry while he rang his loud dinner bell and shouted, "Bible School! Bible School!" Perhaps a hundred or more children followed to the door of the local sanctuary and marched in while Joe played "Onward Christian Soldiers" on the piano and stood waiting for Larry to give them directions. One child was handed an American flag to display while another led the group in reciting the pledge to the American flag. Then a child would lead in the pledge to the Christian flag. Immediately another child was given an open Bible, which was held high as another child was chosen to lead in the pledge to the Bible. Prayer time was next and eager children held up their hands so they could be given a turn to mention a prayer request. Larry opened the prayer with, "Dear Jesus," which was followed by the children repeating the greeting word for word. He prayed more phrases, which the children repeated and taught them to pray to Jesus.

Children learned and loved to sing songs such as "Every Day with Jesus", "Give Me Oil in My Lamp", "Thank You Lord for Saving My Soul" and many more. The children enjoyed the mission stories accompanied by visuals using the flannel graphs, simple crafts which they made to help remember the Bible truths that they learned and above all, the scriptures they memorized. The time was packed and well planned. After a short Bible challenge at the end, Larry had the children to place their two fists together and he compared it to their hearts which they could open and close when inviting Jesus to come in and live in their hearts. Holding their fists together in front of a heart, the children prayed for Jesus to come into their hearts and live there, again using the leader-repeat method. Only God knows how many children genuinely accepted Jesus into their hearts as the result of Larry and Joe's endeavors.

Larry loved children and they loved him. He could laugh with them and yet be stern and they were not offended. They respected and obeyed him. Many parents were won to Christ through their children. Joe told about one sermon that Larry preached to the children about Judas selling Jesus for thirty pieces of silver. Larry had gone to the bank before the sermon and gotten thirty silver dollars. When he came to the point in his sermon where Judas returned the money and threw it on the floor, Larry forcefully threw his thirty silver dollars out on to the wooden floor making a loud noise. The children were obviously touched by this story. Larry continued to bring home his point by stating that some people sell Jesus for much less, a little white lie, or for other things that they knew were sinful.

Larry became involved in activities developing his God-given talents for his calling. He was involved in many inspiring experiences sponsored by the preacher boy class in which up to a thousand boys went out on weekends to preach in pulpits and on street corners in areas within a hundred mile radius of the university. Students went alone or in groups, passing out tracts, witnessing for the Lord, playing, singing and were involved in practical ministerial activities, learning through these experiences with fellow classmates. Each week they returned to their studies tired but inspired, because they had ministered for the Lord and rejoiced in their accomplishments for His glory.

Larry was a master teacher. He taught by example and encouraged participation. He never tired of building the fire in the stove in preparation for church or children's meetings. He gave of himself in many ways. Larry did not consider church work to be a schedule of meetings or appointments, but a 24/7 always-on-call service for the Lord.

Prayer and Outreach Focus

Remember to pray for the college students from your church. Send them emails or keep in touch with them on a regular basis letting them know that you care about them and are remembering them in prayer. Send them a care package if they are away in college. They will be making critical decisions about their careers, marriage and spiritual matters during their college years. They need your prayers.

Margaret with her roommates at Holmes College of the Bible 1954.
(From left to right: Corene Caudle, Anne Brewton, Fannie Lowe and Margaret Rogers).

Holmes Bible College Class of 1955.

THE WELCH DAILY NEWS

West Va.   APR 7   1955

SALUTATORIAN — Miss Margaret Bishop, (above), of Caretta, will be salutatorian at commencement exercises at Holmes Bible College, Greenville, S. C. She is the daughter of Mr. and Mrs. Jesse F. Bishop of Caretta, and plans to go to India as a missionary. It has been her ambition since childhood to teach children and work in Vacation Bible Schools.

Margaret Bishop Salutatorian Holmes College of the Bible 1955.

Chapter Five

Family Illnesses

Mabel Bishop's Illness

Is any of you sick? He should call the elders of the church to pray over him and anoint him with oil in the name of the Lord. And the prayer offered in faith will make the sick person well: the Lord will raise him up. . . (James 5:14-15).

Few events shape the character of an individual and family like a critical or terminal illness. While Margaret was a student at Holmes College of the Bible during her second year, she received the news that her mother was gravely ill with tuberculosis and that she had been sent to the Pine Crest Sanitarium in Beckley, West Virginia. [1]

Margaret immediately offered to return home to help to care for her family. Jesse wrote her a letter and emphatically insisted that God had called her to the ministry and that she was to continue her education. She received a letter from her mother shortly thereafter. Her mother also insisted that Margaret remain at Holmes and continue her education. Aileen had gone to Mount Airy, North Carolina to stay with her Uncle Frank and Aunt Ima to work in a nearby hosiery mill after graduating from high school. Marie was a senior in high school. Yvonne was a freshman in high school and Jim was ten years old.

After Mabel was taken to the sanitarium, two ladies from the Health Department came to advise the family about sterilizing everything in the house to avoid spreading the tuberculosis germ. They did not have dishwashers then. Yvonne told about having to fill a large galvanized tub with water and boiling the water on top of the stove with bleach to wash all of their dishes and eating utensils after every meal. These precautions were valuable training for Margaret when she was later exposed to disease and unsanitary conditions in a third world country. The nurses from the health department came to their home routinely to test each of the family members for tuberculosis.

While Mabel was isolated from the family for over two and a half years, she continued to maintain her faith in God and to share her faith with those around her. She interceded for her family and for the lost patients dying around her daily. She prayed for her healing and for the healing of others. She prayed that she would be faithful and that like Job she would come forth as gold. She wrote about her diagnosis in her journal.

In the latter part of 1953, I began to feel my health was just ebbing away. I did not have an appetite and I continued to lose weight. I tried to rest all I could but didn't seem to get any better. I went to the doctor and he gave me some medications. I just didn't respond.

Aileen was working in Mount Airy, North Carolina and had been laid off. She came home and was so much help to me. We made preparations for the holidays. Margaret came home from Holmes Bible College for the holidays. It was so nice to have the family together.

I went back to the doctor after the holidays and he sent me to the hospital for some tests. The doctor called me to his office after many tests and told me that he had some bad news. He told me that I had tuberculosis and told me that I would need to go to the sanitarium in Beckley, West Virginia. It would be about two weeks before they could get me a room.

I went home and received a letter from my brother saying that my dad was very ill. On January 24, 1953 the funeral director came to our door and told me that my dad had passed. This was one of the saddest days of my life. We went to North Carolina to pay our last respects. Oh these were trying days. My dad was one of the best friends I ever had. It seemed my heart inside me was crushed.

On February 1, 1954, I entered Pine Crest Sanitarium in Beckley, West Virginia. I was put in a room with a lady that smoked and talked excessively. I got so homesick. I would worry and turn my face to the wall and cry and pray. God opened my eyes and helped me to get hold of myself. I began to think of my precious husband and my children. I must try to be cheerful and help those around me. I read my Bible. I slept most nights with God's word cradled in my arms praying for my family and asking God not to let one of them ever fail him. [2]

It is interesting that smoking was not only permitted, but encouraged in the sanitarium. Doctors proclaimed the benefits of cigarette smoking from the 1930s to the 1950s. The medical profession taught that deeply inhaling menthol cigarette smoke helped to heal the lungs. Doctors recommended smoking for individuals with asthma and tuberculosis. Tobacco companies often used doctors in their advertisements with slogans like, "More doctors smoke Camels than any other cigarette" (Camel, 1945-47).[3] "Physicians say Luckies are your throat protection against irritation and cough." Lucky Strikes claimed that this advertisement in the 1930s was based on the research of 20,878 physicians.[4] Philip Morris claimed in 1936 that a group of doctors had proved conclusively that patients who switched to their cigarettes no longer had signs of throat irritation and were definitely improved. In 1941, Philip Morris claimed that eminent medical authorities recognized the benefits of their product for the nose and throat. In 1948, Philip Morris stated, "leading nose and throat specialists suggest Philip Morris."[5]

Riviera cigarettes were marketed as a cure for bronchial and asthmatic disorders. In the 1950s they advertised their cigarettes with soothing menthol without the taste of medicine. Dr. Max Cutler, a cancer surgeon was quoted as saying "the blanket statements appearing in the press that there is a direct and causative relation between smoking cigarettes and cancer of the lung are an absolutely unwarranted conclusion"[6] (New York Times, April 14, 1954). In this same article, Dr. Heuper at the National Cancer Institute stated, "If excessive smoking actually plays a role in the production of lung cancer, it seems to be a minor one."[7] The Brown & Williamson website documents advertisements and testimonials from doctors who encouraged patients to smoke.

Mabel had heard Pentecostal Holiness preachers preach against cigarette smoking. These preachers taught that smoking was harmful and defiled the temple of the Holy Spirit. At that time preachers really did not have any medical evidence to substantiate their claims. They were ahead of their time and are to be commended for their stand.

The woman that was in the room with Mabel that smoked had been brought up in the Pentecostal Holiness Church and had heard similar preaching. Unfortunately, she chose to accept popular views and died a short time after she entered the sanitarium like many other patients who smoked.

There were 600 patients at the Pine Crest Sanitarium and Mabel was on the sixth floor. Jesse, Yvonne and Jim would come every Saturday to see her. Marie got married the first summer that her mother was in the sanitarium and went to Texas to be with her husband who was in the Army. Mabel wrote about having to talk to her son from a sixth floor window while he waited down in the parking lot. Children under 12 years of age were not allowed to visit.

Mabel used every opportunity she could to witness to the other patients and to pray with them when they were discouraged. She told of one lady who was a school teacher in the area and had been sent to Pine Crest. This lady mocked preachers who came to visit and was antagonistic toward Christians. Mabel continued to pray for her. After her condition had continued to worsen and she had endured numerous surgeries, she began to ask Mabel to pray with her. Mabel wrote,

> I talked to her about being born again. One day it was raining and we met for prayer and I said, "Jesus wants to save you today." We hadn't prayed very long until she began laughing and I looked at her and she had a smile on her face and tears were streaming down her cheeks. I said, "Do you believe that God has saved you?" With a gleam in her eyes she said, "Yes. I love everybody and I have joy in my heart. Then she just let the hallelujahs roll! What joy! She didn't live long after this experience. She became very ill after that and her mother came to be with her. In her last moments, she looked at her mother and smiled and said, "Mother, Jesus is very near." Then she passed on to that great beyond. I heard her calling my name in her dying moments but the nurses would not let me go to her. Her mother came in and thanked me for leading her daughter to God. The fruit of the righteous is a tree of life and he that winneth souls is wise (Proverbs 11:30 KJV).[8]

Mabel wrote that she prayed and read her Bible consistently. She tried to keep her spirits up and to encourage those around her. Still there were days when she began to worry about her condition and her family. She would sometimes become discouraged about the fact that she was a shut in. She wrote about having to miss her daughter's graduations, two daughter's weddings and her husband's ordination ceremony. She wrote, "But there is one appointment that I will not miss. I will not miss the great marriage super of the Lamb. I want my vessel to be filled with oil that I might be ready to meet Him."[9]

Thanksgiving, 1954 was one of those times when Mabel began to feel discouraged. Jesse, Yvonne and Jim went to see her and stayed for the two hour visitation period. They brought her flowers from the Coalwood Pentecostal Holiness Church and tried to cheer her spirit. She so much wished that she could be at home to prepare one of her Thanksgiving feasts for her family. She talked about the nurses bringing her a beautiful Thanksgiving dinner with all of the trimmings. She said, "If I could just have someone to share this wonderful meal with me." She thought of a friend down the hall and thought that she must be lonely too and asked the nurse if she and Mrs. Triplett could eat their Thanksgiving dinner together. The nurse allowed Mrs. Triplett to come to her room and they enjoyed their Thanksgiving meal and fellowship together. After this dinner she wrote, "May we have grace to never question God." Isaiah 45:3 what a promise![10]

During the Thanksgiving season that year she wrote a poem that she called the "Shut-in's Prayer":

Last night the moon pulled an anchor and sailed down the Milky Way.
The moon peeped through a sanitarium window where a lonely shut- in lay.
Then the moon seemed to shine much brighter.

Each star seemed to nod its head.
And the night became more peaceful when they heard what the shut-in said.
Dear God, way up there in heaven I earnestly pray to Thee.
You'll answer my prayer now won't You?
Lay a healing hand on me.
Dear Father, the world forgets me. I've been a shut in for so long.
I need Your lovely dear Jesus.
Instill in my heart a song.
I trust that I'm not asking too much of Thy heavenly wealth.
When I so humbly pray, You to give me back my health.
The moon sailed on her journey.
The stars twinkled from above.
The shut-in drifted off to dream land.
What is greater than God's love? (Mabel Bishop)
"Where is God my maker who giveth songs in the night?" (Job 35:10 KJV)[11]

On April 28, 1955 the doctor diagnosed Mabel as having pneunoperitonum. A pneunoperitonum is the presence of air or gas in the peritoneal cavity in the lungs that causes a rupture to occur in the lung wall. The lung may collapse. This can occur spontaneously or as the result of a surgical procedure or treatment. Sometimes a controlled procedure involves pumping air into the peritoneal cavity to aid in pulmonary function. Apparently in Mabel's case, the pneunoperitonum was possibly caused from some of the treatments that she had been given for tuberculosis. She became despondent for a few days after this diagnosis. She talked about a lady from Oak Hill, West Virginia coming to pray with her and about the people from the Coalwood, West Virginia Pentecostal Holiness Church that continued to lift her up in prayer and encouraged her with cards and flowers.

Mabel had a dream while she was in the sanitarium that she had been healed and that she was at home playing with a yard full of her grandchildren. She wrote to Jesse that she believed that she was going to be healed and that she would live to see her grandchildren.

Mabel was released from the Pine Crest Sanitarium near the end of 1956. She lived almost another 30 years and saw not only her 13 grandchildren, but several great-grandchildren born before her death. She was able to attend many of their graduations, weddings and her own 50th anniversary celebration.

The children seemed to have saved up a host of special events for their mother's homecoming. Marie brought home the first grandchild, Patty. Yvonne graduated from Big Creek High School. Margaret and Yvonne both had wedding plans in the making and were elated that their mother would be able to attend these events. Larry and Margaret were married in January, 1957 and Ralph and Yvonne were married in July, 1957.

Larry's Brother
When Larry was six years old his youngest brother, Douglas, was diagnosed with nephritis (Bright's disease). At that time, there were no treatments or medications for nephritis. Larry talked about walking the floor and holding little Douglas when he cried. Some nights he would stay up all night walking the floor and praying for him. The entire family was crushed when he died. Larry would still cry when he would talk about little Douglas many years later. This loss was to shape Larry in to the compassionate, caring person that he became as an adult. He always had a special empathy for children that were suffering in any way and did everything that he could to help alleviate their pain and suffering. The stories that Larry and his brothers heard their mother tell about her experiences in an orphanage as a child were to also influence

Larry's life and ministry. Larry always had an empathy with children in orphanages and children that were from broken homes. He tried to be a father to the fatherless as the scriptures admonish.

Prayer and Outreach Focus

Every church has at least one person who is suffering with a terminal illness. The scriptures admonish us to pray for the sick. We should also do what we can to minister to their needs and to help their families during these times of crisis.

Part II

Pastoring & Teaching

Chapter Six

Early Careers

He makes me lie down in green pastures; he leads me beside quiet waters.
(Psalms 23:2).

When Margaret returned home from college, she learned that a substitute teacher was needed at McDowell Elementary School in McDowell, West Virginia. She applied for this job and was hired as a 5th grade substitute for the year. She also obtained her minister's license and began pastoring the Pentecostal Holiness Church in Yukon, West Virginia.

Larry went to Mitchelltown, Virginia to pastor the Mitchelltown Pentecostal Holiness Church (now Lifeline Ministries)[1] in 1952. Pastor Frank Neff now pastors this church and it is now one of the largest churches in the Alleghany Highlands. Some of the children and grandchildren of the people that opposed the church in the beginning are now the backbone of the church.

John Woodzell, whose mother, Josephine Woodzell was a charter member of the Mitchelltown Pentecostal Holiness Church believes that Larry was the first fulltime pastor.[2] Up to that point the church had shared a pastor with the Covington Pentecostal Holiness Church which was a large flourishing church at that time. The entire country and Bath County especially had not recovered from the depression, and War II. The church was very poor with perhaps as few as 20 to 30 active members. Most of the members who had jobs worked for wealthy land owners who paid very poor wages. One pastor who served both charges for six years told John Woodzell later that the largest offering he received from Mitchelltown during the time that he pastored there was $5.00. Josephine Woodzell was the church secretary and treasurer. During those early years, John recalls times when the light bill would be less than $2.00 and his mother had to struggle to come up with that much. There was no parsonage, as prior pastors lived at the parsonage in Covington. Larry had a room with Mrs. Priscilla Rodgers who worked and lived outside her home. She fixed meals for Larry on her day off and he had kitchen privileges when she was gone.[3]

Mrs. Rodger's was a cook for Sargent Shriver and his family in Hot Springs, Virginia. She could prepare the most elegant meals with the greatest of ease. She prepared a prune cake for Larry's birthday that became his favorite. She gave him the recipe and after he married Margaret, he would ask her to prepare the traditional prune cake each year for his birthday.

Mrs. Rodgers was a strong person and had endured many difficulties in life. She was persistent and always seemed to have the grace to deal with any situation. The children of the members who were there during the time that Larry served the Mitchelltown Pentecostal Holiness Church remember that some of the families invited him for his evening meals at their homes and that he could not drive and did not have a car when he arrived in Mitchelltown. John Woodzell recalls seeing Larry walking all over the community.[4]

During the time that Larry pastored the Mitchelltown Pentecostal Holiness Church, Mrs. Rodger's sister, Josephine Woodzell taught him how to drive. Josephine had two sons and was not intimidated by any challenge. Her husband told her that she could never teach Larry to drive because he was too hard-headed. Larry decided that he had finally mastered the task and was ready to get his license and to find his first car. Larry's dad had purchased an Oldsmobile that Joe had driven his last year of high school and Larry worked out a deal with his dad to get this car while he was in Mitchelltown. Larry enjoyed spending time with John and Billy while Josephine cooked him some of her delicious meals. Margaret continues to make Josephine's whole wheat bread recipe.

Larry had a wonderful personality and made a multitude of friends as he moved about the county. As a young pastor, Larry dealt with some people who were set in their ways, perhaps a bit radical. John Woodzell remembers Larry sharing with him much later that he wanted to bring a very good choir from a local black church to sing at Mitchelltown and he almost got tarred and feathered for even suggesting such a thing. When Larry dealt with these crises he sought the Holy Spirit's guidance and as a result he was able to resolve many issues and to win the favor of the people. He was regarded by the members as being personable, intelligent and a diligent worker.[5]

Larry and a few dedicated members, mostly older ladies managed to move the church into a level of respectability and substance never enjoyed before his tenure and did so without compromising God's word or will in any way. John Woodzell commented that he believed that much of the groundwork for the church's success today was laid under Larry Roger's leadership and under very difficult situations.[6]

Larry enjoyed fellowship with the Laws, the McDaniels, the Pritts, the Schaeffer's and other families in the Mitchelltown Pentecostal Holiness Church. De Law Seawright remembers him taking her along with a group of other teenagers to visit Emmanuel College for the first time. De was later to become the women's residence hall advisor and taught psychology at Emmanuel College. She served on the Emmanuel College board for a number of years.

De Seawright commented that the most memorable thing that she and others remembered about Larry's pastorate in Mitchelltown was his work with the young people "... a breath of fresh air. He seemed to know how to relate to all. . . in the church and in the community. The attendance increased during Larry's time at Mitchelltown. Larry seemed to be able to concentrate on the positive in people. He laughed a lot. . . a hearty laugh."[7]

John Woodzell also commented on Larry's work with the young people. He talked about how difficult it was for young people in those early days especially if they played sports or engaged in other extracurricular activities. Much of this was brought on by people that tried to make religion a set of negative rules and not Biblical truths. Larry talked about going to the mission field often. He wanted to learn all that he could while he was in Bath County about farming so that he could become self-sufficient and share agricultural knowledge in third world countries as a missionary.

De talked about Larry coming to visit the Law farm. "He was not country."[8] He was eager to learn about life on the farm and enjoyed Earl Law's farming demonstrations. Earl Law taught him all about milking the cows, feeding sheep and pigs, cutting wood, making hay, cleaning the barn, planting and weeding a vegetable garden and everything else about farm life.

Larry always wanted to dress and act in a professional manner. The Laws remember him showing up to work on the farm wearing a neatly pressed and starched white shirt and tie and his wing-tip shoes. De commented that the cows were not impressed.

Henry McDaniel had a greenhouse that he had constructed over one of the mineral springs in Warm Springs. The spring consistently stayed at 98.6 degrees year round even in the cold, Bath County winters.

Henry could grow beautiful produce year round and would sell his produce to the local Mick-or-Mack. Henry was a perfectionist and could tell Larry all of the secrets to producing the largest crop yields and highest quality vegetables. Larry enjoyed talking with Henry about raising garden vegetables while Francis would cook a fine chicken dinner with fresh vegetables and her trade mark cherry pie.

The Shaffiers had a hunting camp where family members and friends came to visit and to hunt and fish. They would host the annual church home coming and other church events before the church had a fellowship hall. There were always plenty of hunting tales and wonderful fellowship at the Shafffier's.

Prayer and Outreach Focus

Pray for the young adults in your church, neighborhood and where you work. Pray that God will give them the guidance and direction that they need in their lives. Be available as a mentor to young adults that you know.

Margaret Bishop in her early 20s.

Chapter Seven

Marriage
Oh Shenandoah

He who finds a wife finds what is good and receives favor from the Lord (Proverbs 18:22).

Larry moved to Shenandoah, Virginia to accept a pastorate at the Shenandoah Pentecostal Holiness Church in 1956. Larry announced to the church that he was going to get married in January, 1957. Everyone wanted to know all about his fiancée. He told them that she was a 200-pound woman and had brilliant red hair. When he brought Margaret to church with him, one older gentleman remarked that he must have brought the wrong woman because she did not look like the woman that he had described.

The couple spent their honeymoon in Charleston, South Carolina where they visited local tourist attractions and went to hear a lecture by DeVern Fromke the German theologian who wrote the book, *Come Hither. . .God Is Calling His Blood-Bought Children to be Overcomers.*

Larry's brother, Joe moved to Shenandoah to help Larry with the music at the church. Joe taught music at Elkton High School. Margaret taught the fifth grade at Shenandoah Elementary School, just across the street from the parsonage.

Larry was always known for being resourceful. While he pastored in Shenandoah he acquired 5 goats, rabbits, 12 turkeys, 30 chickens and other livestock to provide milk and meat for their household. One of the goats, Hortense was pregnant when they got her and soon little Willoughby was born.

The Shenandoah winter was too severe for the young turkeys to survive outside so Larry brought them inside to stay in the bathroom for the winter so that they would not freeze. He built cages for the rabbits and a pen for the chickens with a roof. Once during a storm, Larry called Margaret and Joe to collect the chickens and to put them in their pin to protect them during the storm. Margaret and Joe quickly decided that collecting chickens was not their calling in life. A neighbor called one night in the middle of the night to report that the rabbits were out and Larry had to chase rabbits around the neighborhood until he had caught them all and put them back in their cages.

The turkeys could not be contained and often flew over the fence to annoy the neighbors. The goats were the most difficult animals to manage. One day they decided to go to school and Margaret had to call Larry to retrieve them. The next door neighbor, Granny Smith called one day to report that Hortense was eating the bark off of her apple tree. Margaret pulled up Hortense's stake to move her away from the apple tree. Hortense decided to take off at lightning speed with Margaret in tow. Margaret was determined not to let Hortense go. She held tightly to her rope while Hortense drug her for some distance, destroying her stockings and leaving multiple scrapes and bruises. She eventually staked Hortense away from Granny Smith's apple tree.

It took three people to milk Hortense. Joe would hold her head. Margaret held little Willougby to keep her from drinking the goat's milk and Larry would milk Hortense.

The first spring that they were in Shenandoah, Larry built a fence around the parsonage property and planted a large garden to provide produce for his family and to share with neighbors and friends at the church. They did not have a freezer so they rented space at a local freezer locker for their meat and frozen goods in Elkton. The chickens and the rabbits were killed and bagged for freezing. When they moved, they purchased some dry ice to transport the meat from Shenandoah to Charleston, West Virginia, where they rented a freezer locker.

Madison College

Margaret continued her education at Madison College (now James Madison University) in Harrisonburg, Virginia while they were in Shenandoah. She took a remedial reading course at Madison College that motivated her to become a remedial reading teacher. The skills that she acquired in this course and throughout her career would be instrumental in helping her as a teacher of English as a second language when she later became a missionary in Morocco. Margaret continued her education at Marshall University when she and Larry moved to Saint Albans, West Virginia. She earned Bachelor's and Master's degrees in remedial reading at Marshall University.

New Churches

While Larry and Margaret were in Shenandoah, they helped to start two other churches in Luray and Charlottesville, Virginia. The Charlottesville Pentecostal Holiness Church started in a tent. Margaret went to preach at the Charlottesville Pentecostal Holiness Church one evening accompanied by Leland and Mary Crawford. While she was speaking, everyone suddenly noticed an uninvited visitor. A skunk appeared from under the podium and paraded across the stage. The skunk was not the blessing that the congregants were seeking that night and they were quite relieved when she decided to wonder out in the woods.

Prayer and Outreach Focus

Pray for young couples in your church. They are facing many struggles and adjustments and need your prayers. Especially pray for young couples who have indicated that God has called them to some area of ministry or missions. These individuals need special help and grace.

Larry Rogers and Margaret Bishop's wedding.

Chapter Eight

Saint Albans, West Virginia-Miracle Acres

Is anything too hard for the Lord? (Genesis 18:14).

Larry and Margaret moved to Saint Albans, West Virginia on January 15, 1959 to start a new church. David Kibler from Shenandoah went with Larry as he drove his old Oldsmobile to Saint Albans with a small trailer carrying all of their belongings. Margaret was determined to go with him as soon as possible even though she lamented the fact that she would have to leave her school children in the middle of the school year.

Saint Albans is a suburb of Charleston, West Virginia. The beautiful Kanawha Valley and the surrounding area is the most densely populated area in West Virginia. Walter Lee Wood, Jr. had started a church in Charleston, West Virginia that was showing steady growth and it seemed logical to expand to the neighboring cities. The Woods and the Rogers enjoyed their many times of fellowship together while they were in the Kanawha Valley.

Margaret soon found a job in the Kanawha County public schools. Larry bought a business that produced CO_2 cylinders and sold the CO_2 to local businesses for making syrup for carbonated sodas. The Virginia Conference of the Pentecostal Holiness Church (now the Appalachian Conference) purchased a small house on Abney Street that was to serve as a church and parsonage. The first Sunday school was held on March 1, 1959 in the parsonage. The church held their first revival in April with evangelist, J.B. Daugherty.

The first converts during this revival were Olen Daugherty and his wife, Jean. The Daugherty's became charter members of the church and Olen later became a minister. Olen had the distinction of being the first secretary-treasurer, first Sunday school superintendent and first trustee of the church. He and his family were instrumental in establishing the Pentecostal Holiness Church in Belpre, Ohio. While living in Ohio, Olen began to study for his ministerial credentials and later became pastor in Ellenboro, West Virginia for the United Methodist Church. His son, Ronnie Daugherty pastors a United Methodist Church in Bradshaw, West Virginia.

Joe Rogers moved to the area and married Harriet Green. Joe assisted Larry with the music. Two families started to come to the church. Margaret trained two teenage girls to use flannel graphs to help with the children's ministry. Margaret's brother, Jim came to spend the summer with Larry and Margaret prior to his senior year in high school. Larry and Margaret were still in the first house in Saint Albans on Abney Street. Larry had decided to put a basement under the house for them to use for the church. He asked

Jim to dig the basement out by hand. Jim spent all summer working and digging out the basement. The conference board did not think that this space would be adequate and began searching for other property.

In the fall of 1963 the conference purchased property on the other side of town in the Marlang Subdivision. The conference donated a temporary aluminum structure for the church. The ground breaking for the church was held in 1965. A new church board was elected and the church began to grow.

The Rogers moved to a two bedroom house on a corner lot. The dirt that Jim dug out the previous summer had to be put back under the house where the basement had been dug before the house could be sold. The dirt had been used to level the yard, so they actually had to haul in tons and tons of dirt to replace the dirt that he had worked so diligently to dig out the previous summer.

Jim's interest in science began in the 9th grade at Coalwood Junior High School in Coalwood, West Virginia. His science teacher encouraged him to create something for a science project and he chose to build a rocket. He says that his display did not get the attention that Homer Hickam's received about two years later at Big Creek High School, but he enjoyed the project. Homer Hickam was one year ahead of Jim in school.

Near the end of summer school Jim found a part-time job at Kroger in South Charleston. Jim asked Larry and Margaret if he could invite their cousin, Tom Bishop to come to Saint Albans so that he could attend college. Larry and Margaret agreed to let Tom come to stay with them. Jim wrote Tom and persuaded him to join him. Tom came to Saint Albans and found a job at the Saint Albans Kroger. Jim and Tom enrolled at West Virginia State University in the fall. Jim completed two years there and then transferred to West Virginia Tech in Montgomery, West Virginia where he resided during the week and returned to Saint Albans for the weekends. He continued to work at Kroger. The church was in its infancy and Jim and Tom were incorporated into everything. Tom continued to live in Saint Albans and graduated from West Virginia State. He then moved to Morgantown for one year where he worked toward a Master's degree in accounting.

Jim and Tom both have pleasant memories of the five years that they spent with Larry and Margaret in St. Albans. They had wrestling matches in the living room. Once one of them was thrown across a coffee table and a lamp was destroyed. They went to school, worked and came home to have fun. Once they came home from work and the church had just finished an ice cream supper. Tom and Jim began to dig into the ice cream with everyone else. Someone said, "This churn is full, but whoever made it didn't put in enough sugar." Tom looked at Jim with a smile and ran for the sugar bowl. After he had consumed about a half-gallon, Tom said, "You know, this ice cream really wasn't up to par."

Tom and Jim remember some of the cooking episodes or experiments. One of their most memorable tales was when Larry decided to make grape juice in a pressure cooker. The valve got stopped up and the lid blew off spewing grape juice all over the freshly-painted kitchen.

Sunday dinner was always special. It was the only day that Tom and Jim did not have to worry about school or work. One Sunday Margaret had prepared a beautiful spread with a pot roast, vegetables, salad and of course biscuits. As they gathered around the table Margaret was setting the food on the table, but stumbled with the biscuits and dumped them on the floor. She hurriedly cleaned them up, but Tom and Jim persuaded her that they would still be fine. They said the blessing and Jim put some Italian dressing on his salad. Jim passed the dressing to Larry, but failed to put the lid on tight. Larry liked his dressing well mixed, so he shook it violently. Suddenly the lid came off and Italian dressing flew all over Larry and all the way up to the ceiling. Margaret was just getting seated when the dressing bomb went off and she commented, "This meal is like slopping the hogs!" Both of these young men contributed heavily to the projects that Larry and Margaret were involved in at the new church. They helped with the music, taught classes or whatever they were asked to do.

Another favorite tale was the time that Larry went to deliver some $_{CO_2}$ cylinders to a gentleman on a hot day and he offered him something cold to drink. Larry politely took the drink that he offered him and quickly guzzled it down to quench his thirst. The kind gentleman saw that he was quite thirsty so he brought him a second glass. Larry guzzled the second glass and the gentleman went to get him yet another. When he came back with the third glass, Larry asked what all was in this wonderful drink. The gentleman proceeded to tell him that this concoction contained various alcoholic spirits. Larry left as soon as he could politely get away and took off home. When he opened the door, he burst in with the announcement, "Margaret, I'm drunk! I'm drunk!"

Jim and Tom worked at the local Kroger grocery store to earn funds for college. Jim met his wife Brenda Rigsby in Nitro, West Virginia while he was there and Tom met his wife, Connie Wiley from White Sulfur Springs, West Virginia. Tom and Connie remained in the area after Tom graduated and moved in a house next to Larry and Margaret. They continued to assist Larry and Margaret in the church and Larry and Margaret enjoyed many happy times together with Tom and Connie and their two daughters, Lisa and Lena.

It would seem that the challenges of two full-time careers, pastoring a church and constructing a church building would have been sufficient for this young ambitious couple. They seemed to be drawn to far greater challenges as their ministries expanded in the Kanawha Valley.

The Pentecostal Holiness Church Housing Corporation

"Miracle Acres"

In the 1960s many federally subsidized housing projects were springing up in cities across the country to provide housing for individuals in poverty. A project was proposed in Saint Albans and the local government leaders wanted to cooperate with a church in the area that would manage the housing complex. This was to be one of the first faith-based ministry projects of its kind. These leaders first approached an Episcopalian congregation and then other local congregations. None of them agreed to this venture. The Housing and Urban Development (HUD) official stopped in a local block factory and a man there suggested that he talk with Larry Rogers about the proposed housing project. When the HUD official approached Larry he invited him to come to the next church board meeting to explain his proposal.

The HUD official explained his proposal and asked if the Saint Albans Pentecostal Holiness Church would be willing to assist in this endeavor. There was total silence. No one was familiar with this type of project and they could not conceive of all the implications for their church. Larry asked the HUD representative to leave the room while he discussed the project with the church board. Larry told them that if this was of the Lord that it would provide a means for the church to reach the families that they had been trying to reach in their neighborhood. He saw it as an opportunity to grow the church as well as to provide housing for needy people. He encouraged the board to allow the HUD representative to explain the project further.

Larry invited the HUD representative back in the room and he showed them blue prints of the project and explained the legal details. The project would involve constructing 100 units of housing that would be sponsored by the federal government. The church would manage the project and after forty years the property would belong to the Saint Albans Pentecostal Holiness Church (now Trinity Fellowship). The church board voted and unanimously agreed to participate in the project.

The Pentecostal Holiness Church Housing Corporation was established on January 9, 1969. The church board named the project, Miracle Acres because they felt that it was a miracle that the Lord had given them such an opportunity. Larry Rogers saw his prayer answered with the establishment of the corporation. This endeavor was a part of his ministry to help provide housing for families living in substandard accommodations in the western Saint Albans area. This giant step for a small, struggling church met a critical need for 100 families.

The financing was provided by the Prudential Insurance Company and the Department of Housing and Urban Development. The original cost of the project was $1,500,000. The project was financed for 40 years and the note was paid in full by the 40th anniversary date. The housing project was deeded to the Saint Albans Pentecostal Holiness Church in 2009. The current value of the property is now estimated to be over twice the original construction cost even in a depressed economy. Since August 1970, the Pentecostal Holiness Housing Corporation has been meeting the needs of low income families.

The Articles of Incorporation were reestablished on March 17, 1978 so that it would become a non-stock, nonprofit organization, thus qualifying as a 501-c3 corporation with the Internal Revenue Service. Many improvements have been made through the years under the direction of dedicated management, employees, board members and the church family. Highly capable and competent employees have dedicated their services and continue to dedicate themselves to the housing project business and ministry.

Larry hired two secretaries, Sandie Bowen and Lois Turner to assist with all of the administrative duties of the project. Jim and Ruth Caperton were some of the early members of the church and they offered many hours of labor. Later, Ruth Caperton's daughter, Karen Adkins, became the project manager in the office and still maintains that position. Connie Bishop also helped with many of the office duties. There were many other volunteers from the church who were always ready to help and to minister to the needs of the residents of Miracle Acres.

Amandaville, the rat and roach-infested slum area that had previously surrounded the church was cleared out and the grateful families moved in to their new homes. They were excited about living in homes that had indoor bathrooms, heat and adequate protection from the elements.

Larry and the church board recognized the need for establishing firm policies for dealing with the 100 families that occupied the new units. There were occasions when the police were called to deal with alcohol and drug problems and domestic situations. One time a lady called Larry in the middle of the night and reported that her husband was trying to kill her with a machete. Larry quickly dressed and went over to their apartment and wrestled with the man until he surrendered the machete. This man had a heart attack and Larry went to visit him in the hospital and prayed with him. He and his wife started coming to church after he got out of the hospital and got saved.

On one occasion some of the tenants got together and complained to the Civil Liberties Union and had an article printed in the newspaper. The next day many citizens refuted their charges and praised the work that Larry and the Saint Albans Pentecostal Holiness Church had done to clean up the neighborhood and to improve living conditions for the poor in the area.

Larry counseled many of the individuals in the housing project and led them to a saving knowledge of Jesus Christ. One young man from the project had gone to jail and Larry faithfully visited him while he was incarcerated. When he was released, he presented a lovely painting to Larry that was placed in the Saint Albans Pentecostal Holiness Church.

Larry purchased a van and would go each Sunday and Wednesday evening and get a load of individuals from the housing development to come to church. They started Sunday school programs for the children and classes for the children on Wednesday evenings. They provided food for them and Margaret planned crafts and activities to occupy the children.

During the time that they lived in Saint Albans Larry and Margaret saw numerous children learn about Jesus and some who gave their hearts to the Lord.

Larry and Margaret left the Saint Albans Pentecostal Holiness Church in 1973 to go to Bluefield, West Virginia. The current pastor, the Reverend Billy Griffin commented that "it is through the sacrifices of people like Larry and Margaret Rogers that we enjoy the benefits of an organized body of believers." [1]

Jack and Dot Perdue and their son, Steve, followed the Rogers and continued the work in a most admirable manner.

Larry and Margaret attended the 40th anniversary celebration of the church in 1999 but were not able to attend the 50th anniversary celebration when Miracle Acres was deeded to the church because of Larry's declining physical condition.

Prayer and Outreach Focus

There are poor and disadvantaged people in every community. Pray that God will open doors for your church to minister to the needs of the poor in your community. Pray for those that the Lord sends to your church, that your church will be faithful in meeting their spiritual and physical needs. Pray for guidance, grace and protection for those who work with individuals that are poor in your community.

Ground Breaking 1965

This picture is of our ground breaking ceremony for the first phase of the building of the church around 1965. Those pictured are left to right:

Ralph W. Sharp, Charter member and deacon
Rev. Walter L. Wood, then pastor of P. H. Church in
　　Charleston
Rev. Vernon McGhee, Presbyterian minister
Rev. Laurence Rogers, First pastor
Rev. B. E. Underwood, then Conference Evangelism Director
Rev. Dan L. Sexton, then pastor of Burlington, Ohio P. H.
　　Church (now deceased)
Herbert Lewis, then deacon and church treasurer

Notice the old tin building which was our first building which we worshiped in on the current church property.

(1965) Ground breaking service for the Saint Albans Pentecostal Holiness Church.

Left to right: Ken Kingrea, previous Bishop of the Appalachian Conference of the International Pentecostal Holiness Church, Ruth Caperton, Tony Price and Margaret Rogers; Karen Atkins (Ruth Caperton's daughter) and Pastor Billy Griffin.

Larry speaking at the 40th Anniversary note-burning service at Saint Albans.

Left to right: Larry Rogers, Ray Caperton and Margaret Rogers.

Chapter Nine

Bluefield, West Virginia: Turning Trash into Treasure

Each man should use whatever gift he has received to serve others, faithfully administering God's grace in its various forms (I Peter 4:10).

Larry and Margaret moved to Bluefield, West Virginia in 1973. Unlike their previous pastorate, the Bluefield Pentecostal Holiness Church was an established church. It had been founded in 1917. The congregation moved to its current location in 1945. When Larry and Margaret were asked to go to this church, they were first concerned about the Saint Albans church finding a pastor that could manage both the church and the housing project. When they learned that Jack Perdue was willing to go to Saint Albans, their minds were relieved of this concern.

Larry and Margaret had grown up in the coalfields of West Virginia and Bluefield immediately felt like home. The people in the church warmly greeted them and the Rogers bonded with them and began to immerse themselves in the church's ministries and activities.

Soon after Larry moved to Bluefield, he decided that it was time to replace his worn out Dodge van. The Dodge Maxi van had just come out and Larry decided that this would be the perfect replacement for his old van. Larry knew that Dodge engines were made at the foundry in Radford at that time. He had known people that worked there and he insisted that Dodge was the best because of the attention to quality that the individuals that he knew gave to their work.

Larry also liked the Dodge Maxi van because he could transport more children to church and to youth camp. He would have more space to haul aluminum cans, copper and paper for recycling. Anyone who saw Larry driving around in his Dodge Maxi van never saw it empty. He used this blessing from the Lord to recycle anything that he could in order to use the funds to recycle lives.

Larry collected used computer data cards for recycling and used the money to purchase shoes for needy children at Christmas. He and Margaret would take the children of the church Christmas caroling and would take food and clothing to needy families as they caroled.

The heavy paper helped to weigh down his van in the cold, snowy winters in Bluefield when he would need to go to the hospitals to visit the sick. On one occasion, he learned that one of his members who lived up in the mountains on East Cumberland Road could not get out for church. He took a pick and a shovel and drove to where she lived and dug the road out so that she could come to church. He soon had everyone in the church as well as neighbors and friends saving newspapers and paper products for his projects and to preserve the environment. One lady commented that he would always load that van to the top.

Larry and Margaret assisted with making apple butter each year. They would usually make about 300 quarts of apple butter in an open kettle starting at about 4:00 on a cool, crisp fall morning. They would channel the money into the youth fund and women's ministries projects. Making apple butter was an important fellowship activity as well as a profit making venture. The ladies would cook a large meal on the day that they made the apple butter and everyone would enjoy fellowshipping together. They would use the funds to buy Bibles for children who would ride the van to church, most of whom had never had a Bible.

Another one of Larry's projects was accumulating aluminum cans and copper for recycling to provide money to send the children to the youth camps in West Virginia and to the Maranatha Camp in Dublin, Virginia. During the time that Larry was in Bluefield, West Virginia, he took an active role in planning and participating in the West Virginia camp meeting, the West Virginia camps, the Pentecostal Fellowship of North America, the Bluefield Ministerial Association and served as a board member on the Virginia Conference board. Margaret took an active role in planning the West Virginia camp activities and assisted with meal preparation and crafts. She served on the women's ministries board for the Virginia Conference.

Margaret continued to serve as a reading specialist in the school system and taught foreign students English as a second language. One year she was named the Mercer County Reading Council Reading Teacher of the Year.

The move to Bluefield proved to be providential to Larry and Margaret as both sets of their parents grew older. Jesse and Mabel Bishop had moved to Shawsville, Virginia where they had pastored the Piedmont Pentecostal Holiness Church until they retired. They began to grow feeble in 1984. Mabel had to be hospitalized several times with pneumonia. Margaret was close enough that she could come down on weekends and when they were in the hospital. Mabel died in January, 1985 with congestive heart failure. Jesse had no will to live after her death and he died also with congestive heart failure in June, 1985.

Larry's parents had moved to Dublin, Virginia in the late 70s. Thelma Rogers had to be placed in a nursing home and died in 1988. Larry would come down between services at his church in Bluefield and stay with his father. His father died shortly after his mother.

Prayer and Outreach Focus

What can your church turn to treasure? Your church might have yard sales; recycle paper, plastic, or aluminum. You could use the funds from these projects to support some home or foreign missions project. Pray that the Lord will help your church to be good stewards.

FELLOWSHIP OFFICERS — These are the new officers of the Greater Bluefield-Princeton Chapter of the Pentecostal Fellowship of North American. Shown from left are Rev. H.L. Rogers of the Bluefield Pentecostal Holiness Church, secretary; Rev. Sylvia Hill, treasurer; Rev. Walter Burgess of the Abbs Valley Church of God, vice president; and Rev. Quentin Hughett of the Princeton Pentecostal Holiness Church, president. Absent when the photo was taken was Rev. Ralph Hager, Sr. of the Stoney Ridge Assembly of God, member-at-large.

Bluefield-Princeton Chapter of the Pentecostal Fellowship of North America (Larry Rogers, far left)

READING COUNCIL OFFICERS are installed at the May dinner held at Concord College with Dr. Jerome Niles of Virginia Tech as principal speaker. Left to right are Brenda Grose, past president; Sue Sommer, treasurer; Ruth Boyd, corresponding secretary; Carolyn Sherwood, recording secretary; Margaret Rogers, Reading Teacher of the Year; Carmelite Peters, vice president; Marlin Howell, president, and Dr. Niles. Steve Bailey is the new vice president-elect.

Reading Council Officers (Margaret Rogers, center).

Part III

Call to the House of Berber

Chapter Ten

Call to the House of Berber

I know a man in Christ who fourteen years ago was caught up to the third heaven. Whether it was in the body or out of the body I do not know-God knows. And I know that this man-whether in the body or apart from the body I do not know, but God knows- was caught up to paradise. He heard inexpressible things, things that man is not permitted to tell. I will boast about a man like that but I will not boast about myself, except about my weaknesses (2 Corinthians 12:2-5).

I will never forget the story that Uncle Larry told about the call that he received to go to the House of Berber. I first heard the story in October, 1991. My parents, Ralph and Yvonne Green, mother's brother Jim and his wife, Brenda Bishop, along with Larry and Margaret were gathered in my living room in Franklin Springs, Georgia. Everyone had come down for the King Memorial lecture series at Emmanuel College. There was seldom a moment of silence with two preachers in the house. Larry seemed more quiet than usual. Margaret finally spoke up and said, "Larry has something that he would like to share."

There was an awkward moment of silence as Larry gathered his thoughts. He began by telling about a vision that he had witnessed about two years previously. He saw a person whom he described as the "Ancient of Days." His face glowed as he described this being, the lines in his face and his long snow white hair. He was riding in a chariot and there was an entire group of angels riding with him. This heavenly being commanded him to go to the House of (Barbar) Berber and to affect a blood transfusion. He talked about the face haunting him for days.

He did not know what to think of the vision. He continued to seek God about the meaning of the vision and about the role that he was to play in helping these people. He went to the library and did research. At first he thought that the spelling was "Barbar" like the Barbar of Seville. He could find very little information using this spelling. Finally a librarian suggested that he might try looking under the alternate spelling, "Berber." He determined that the group that the Lord had spoken to him about was an unreached people group in North Africa known as "the Berbers." He decided that he would not share the vision with anyone until he felt the Lord had provided adequate confirmation. He prayed that Margaret would receive a similar vision.

Meanwhile, Margaret had felt that she should take early retirement from her job as a reading specialist in Bluefield, West Virginia. Since they had both felt called to the mission field in their early years, she thought that perhaps they could still serve on the mission field in some capacity. She had sought the Lord about an appropriate opportunity for them to serve on the mission field.

Larry's Dream

The following article appeared in the Virginia Conference Messenger about Larry's vision. Margaret's dream is also included showing that God directed each of them to the same people.[1]

December 1991   Virginia Conference **Messenger**   Page 5

ELEVENTH HOUR LABORERS CALLED TO MISSION FIELD

To our fellow workers in Christ's kingdom:

If you read presumption into this record you miss the entire message. While we can never judge statements prefaced with "God told me," it never removes the question of suspect.

Flesh can't have it, as Isaiah witnessed the seraphim before the throne; of their wings, two covered their faces. From the earliest readings of Jonah, I have questioned how a man could tell on himself, reveal his dark side and present the holiness of God's character. But Jonah does in honesty, as Christ confirms the book, and you understand the Heavenly Father's love for the ancient Iraqi people.

In our earlier years we felt the call to work as missionaries in India. Nothing opened for this venture as India refused visas to new missionaries.

Since that attempt in 1957, our time has been spent pastoring in the conference. Margaret taught in the public school system during this time.

An early retirement package for teachers was offered two years ago and Margaret took advantage of it. It was in her thinking that the Lord would now open up an opportunity to do mission work on one of the fields. Many areas needed someone to teach English. I was not too keen on this idea and reminded her that the Lord had not indicated to me that it was time to leave the present pastorate.

However, the Lord came to me in a dream (vision) one Saturday night two years ago. The dream (vision) was thusly:

I stood by the intersection of Maryland Avenue and Frederick Street near the Bluefield church. I observed a brilliant cloud moving in my direction. It was impossible to take my eyes away. As I watched, the cloud approached as a vehicle transporting a group of what to my knowledge were angels. Everything was very bright. The "cloud of angels" progressed to where I stood and stopped. While I observed, one of the angels came down from the group and stood facing me. He spoke deliberately and clearly, "Go to the House of Barbar and effect a blood transfusion. This is a people determined on

H. L. (Larry) and Margaret Rogers

self-destruction." I became so fascinated with the face of the angel I was really lost if there were anything else said.

I cannot tell anything about the apparel of the angel or his reentry into the cloud. I was aware the vehicle with the heavenly persons swept away as I stood startled. But my full attention was given to the face of the angel that was deeply marked with age lines. It seemed I saw that face for weeks.

After the cloud of angels left, I awakened. It was Saturday night. Where was I to go and how was I to bring about a delivery from a suicide? Nothing remotely made intelligent meaning.

I prayed for months but felt I had no one to discuss it with. Spiritual guidance has, on occasion, been difficult for me. The previous pastorate of fifteen years and the present were moves because of spiritual guidance. So was my Baptism of the Holy Spirit. But in most cases it appeared best to refrain from discussing with others until I was positive. So other than a token question with the thought that there may be some additional information or confirmation, I asked about angels having age lines, or what is the House of Barbar? The Bishop gently answered that he could not identify the House of Barbar, but he would make it a matter of research. So I started research at the local library. Everything turned to a dead-end. Then one day I asked the as-

sistance of the librarian. After about an hour of looking she came to where I was with the stack of books to say, "I believe we are spelling it wrong. In Websters Unabridged Third Edition, after the word **berber** came the spelling **barbar**." Thus the matter opened!

The Berbers (Barbars) are a minority people of the Barbary States in North Africa; Morocco, Algeria, Tunisia, Libya. The people are in all the countries from the west of Egypt to the Atlantic and the edge of the Sahara. They were conquered by Islam and are a part of the Arabic traditions, but are separate in that they hold to a Hamitic language. The Berbers are among the world's unreached people for Christ.

When I had an interview with the chairman of the World Missions Board in July, he inquired, "Are you ready to pull up stakes?" Our two years of multiple questions were compressed into one. The humbling portion of this is the continued flow of confirmations, personal and otherwise.

It appears that at about the same time of the dream one of our missionaries had a group of SAM students witnessing on the streets of London. He was approached by a passerby to inquire about a street address. After the inquiry and making the scene at the address, the man returned to engage the missionary in conversation. He was a BERBER attending a university in London. This ended as a missions contact in Casablanca, Morocco.

When the World Missions director revealed this, he also told of another applicant from the PH Church in Yukon, OK who was called to work among the BERBERS. If we have opportunity coming to your church to itinerate, we would like to share personal confirmations.

We have an awareness that fulfilling the direction of the messenger is a corporate venture and that not only is there great Godly function to fulfilling (as to results, etc.) but there is also great Godly function in the corporate entity itself. So one result is, as we met the World Missions Board and the conclusion is assessed; "What is the Spirit saying to the churches?" I don't know how heaven would measure, but from an earthly view I recall the cloud was well staffed!

H. L. (Larry) and Margaret Rogers

"Eleventh Hour Laborers Called to Mission Field" *Virginia Conference Messenger,* December 1991.

Margaret's Dream

Larry and Margaret went to Regent University to take a 6-week course in reaching unreached people. The instructor encouraged them to choose the country and a city in that country that they would like to reach. They had gone to a special library in Richmond, Virginia and checked out books about Morocco and cities in that country.

As they chose books that were listed as having unreached people, they took them to their room to learn of customs in that area. One that Margaret was reading described the custom of dealing with a young woman found not to be a virgin. As a woman approaches marriage if she is found to not be a virgin, her brothers can take the matter into their own hands and murder their sister. This is their way of saving their family from shame.

During the night Margaret had a dream that she and Larry were in this country. Young people were coming back and forth to see them in their apartment. One day two young people came to their place when Larry was away and told her that they were going to commit suicide. Margaret talked with them at length and prayed with them. When they left she did not feel that she had succeeded in convincing them not to commit suicide. Margaret was disturbed that she did not know where to reach Larry to get his help. She rushed out into the street and found the police and tried to secure their help. They completely ignored her. Margaret told the neighbor to tell Larry where she was if he came back. Then she rushed out to find where the young people were staying. She arrived at their apartment just as Larry came rushing up. They burst into the room to discover that they had already taken their lives. Larry's sad response was, "If we had only been here earlier." Margaret awakened from this dream in tears relating it to Larry. Then she said, "I think this is the place that we should target."

The Dream Fulfilled

Larry and Margaret did target this particular city, Fes, Morocco. One young woman that spoke proficient English befriended them and visited them sometimes two or three times a week. One day she came to Margaret with the sad story that her husband was having an affair with a teacher in the school where he taught out in the country. He only traveled home on the weekend and when he was home, he was very unkind to her. She came to their apartment one day showing bruises where her husband had beaten her. Larry and Margaret prayed with her and let her know that they loved her as they counseled with her. Later she came to tell them that she became so depressed that she had thought of committing suicide. As she started to take her life she thought of Larry and Margaret and how much they loved her and she could not follow through with her suicide plans. [2]

Prayer and Outreach Focus

Pray for those who have felt a call to go to a foreign mission field. Pray for them as they raise their financial support. Pray for a physical and spiritual covering. Pray for their families.

Chapter Eleven

Exploratory Trip to Spain & Morocco

"...I will go to Spain and visit you on the way. I know that when I come to you, I will come in the full measure of the blessing of Christ" (Romans 15:28-29).

Larry and Margaret went on an exploratory trip to Spain and Morocco in July, 1992. The following pages chronicle this visit and their early efforts to learn the culture of the North African region. Margaret kept a journal during this trip and these pages are based on her journal entries.

Norfolk, Virginia—July 9, 1992

Dayton Birt, pastor of Living Word Church in Norfolk took Larry and Margaret to the airport. He agreed to send a fax message to Harold Dalton, mail a package and a mailing list to Pat Johnson in North Carolina who was to distribute a prayer gram. He further offered to watch their car that was left in the church parking lot. Philip and Kelly List joined Larry and Margaret and they departed for Boston. The entire team took the international Sabena line to Brussels, Belgium. This flight took 7.5 hours.

Brussels, Belgium—July 10, 1992[1]

The team had a six hour layover in Brussels. They gathered in one corner of the waiting area and spent some time reading the Bible and praying. Margaret opened a letter that had come from her sister, Aileen and shared it with the group. She had written encouraging words about their exploratory trip. She referred to this trip as a "journey into eternity" and an experience that they would long remember.

They walked through the shops and purchased postcards and learned that the postage was $1.25 for each card. The terminal was extremely hot and they were thirsty. Philip met a couple waiting for the Malaga flight and they gave encouraging words to him. He also met a Spanish instructor who encouraged them to take Arabic.

Malaga, Spain—July 11, 1992[2]

They arrived in Malaga on Friday afternoon and found that the taxi fare to the hotel was $24.00. Philip decided that they could cut the cost by taking the bus. They waited and waited for the bus. Finally the bus came and with the driver's limited English, he motioned for them to get off and pointed in the direction of the hotel. They thought that it must be just around the corner, only to discover that they were lugging their luggage in the heat for three blocks. The hotel was far from inviting. The walls were dark and dirty looking. Sand gritted under their feet as they walked. They were too tired to look further. They checked in and found the beds and bathrooms to be clean. They went out and found a light meal.

The next morning they got together in Philip and Kelly's room for devotions and for planning the day. They decided to find water and a light breakfast before catching the train to Torremolinos. They found water and sweet rolls in a supermarket in a high-rise mall. They rushed to get their luggage from the hotel taking their food with them.

The train station was underground, which meant that they had to drag their luggage down a long flight of stairs. Arriving just minutes before the train was due, they quickly purchased tickets. Then the big rush began. They were to have their first experience at pushing and shoving to get on the train. When the train stopped, everyone made a mad rush for the doors. There was nothing polite about it. They learned later that during this rush, someone had lifted a wallet from a lady's zippered purse in their group. Fortunately, she had put all of her identification and most of her money in her money belt under her blouse.

While on the train they met a Spanish lady that spoke English and enjoyed a conversation with her. After they got off the train the women sat on a park bench with the luggage while the men searched for a hotel. A Dutchman who owned a restaurant spoke English and directed the men to a hotel. He told them that he made the best hamburgers in town. The hotel was very rustic, but immaculate with a receptionist that spoke English and was most congenial. They each went to their rooms, unpacked and relaxed. As they got together to go out to eat they decided to walk down the Mediterranean beach.

There was a winding stairway and sidewalks with shops of all kinds as they descended to the sea. Approaching the beach they saw hundreds of sunbathers, some topless women. After a walk down the beach, they wound their way back up to the Dutchman's café to try his hamburgers. While they were waiting for their order, Philip said, "I hear Christian choruses." They looked over in the city square just beyond the restaurant and there were guitarists, violinists, and a group of singers. They took turns waiting at the table for their orders and going to listen to the music. There were others passing out tracts and invitations to attend the English speaking church. They gave Larry and Margaret a map directing them to the Evangelical Community Church with the English service at 11:00 a.m. They thanked the Lord for making it so easy for them to make contact with a church. They ate their hamburgers which were very good and went out to locate the church. The church was just a nice walk from their hotel.

They exchanged goodnights and returned to the hotel and went to bed by 10:45. They soon learned that no one sleeps in Torremolinos, Spain on Saturday night. As the noise continued, they could not sleep. Margaret decided to get up and read. Larry decided that he would dress and walk out in the streets and see how they were celebrating. He soon returned and had Margaret to dress and go out with him to see the multitudes of young people everywhere. The sidewalk cafes were filled with young people, drinking, singing, playing guitars and clapping. Older people were walking casually around and some sitting on the park benches. Shops were open and people were buying food and cigarettes. Cars were bumper to bumper with horns sounding at 1:00 a.m. They returned to the hotel. The noise continued until 7:00 the next morning. What an experience! Larry and Margaret learned later that Torremolinos is the entertainment center for all of the surrounding towns and that Saturday night is their big night. They avoided being downtown in Torremolinos on Saturday nights after that!

Torremolinos—July 12, 1992[3]

A very sleepy team gathered in Larry and Margaret's room for a breakfast of sweet rolls, bananas and orange juice. Philip checked with the hotel manager and learned that they could leave their luggage stored in closets off from the lobby until they moved out at 7:00 p.m.

They walked to the Evangelical Community Church for the 11:00 worship service. A lovely group had gathered. The Youth with a Mission (YWAM) leader and other missionaries were there. Larry and

Margaret were able to talk to several of them. They gleaned some information about renting apartments. The worship that morning was directed by Pastor Bob, who introduced the speaker who was also the founder of the church and the contractor that had built the church. He went to work with orphans in South America bringing some to Spain to work on a 40-acre farm that he developed after he founded the church. He had sweet corn for sale in the foyer of the church that had been picked on his farm. His wife is a vocalist and sang two songs before he preached. After the service everyone visited until nearly 2:00. No one seemed in a hurry and this was the one time in the week when they were able to see each other.

They ate their Sunday dinner at an outdoor café and returned to the hotel lobby to relax until 7:00. Larry and Margaret were too tired to do any sightseeing. They called two cabs at 7:00 to take them and their luggage to the YWAM Center, Ville Isabel in the El Pinar section of Torremolinos. The director and his wife received them cordially. They showed them to upstairs rooms with individual baths. Outside their door was a veranda with a beautiful view of the city and the Mediterranean Sea. They all went to bed early and slept well.

July 13, 1992

As they went down to breakfast in the YWAM center dining room, Larry and Margaret met a couple working with YWAM on assignment in Fes, Morocco. He was a dark Venezuelan who would not be spotted easily as a foreigner in Morocco. She had a vibrant personality and was on fire for the Lord and both seemed to be dedicated to the cause of winning the Muslims for Christ.

Later at lunch Larry and Margaret met other guests, a young Englishman, who worked as a worship team leader for YWAM and a young Swedish girl that was returning from working at the Expo at the Pavilion Promise. She was traveling alone with her backpack without fear.

The YWAM director gave the team an appointment after lunch. They met the director on the veranda behind the dining area overlooking Malaga Bay. He was most helpful in giving information and instruction from his wealth of experiences and was in no hurry. He talked to Larry and Margaret for three hours. He gave them good advice for their tour of Morocco. He had directed several trips into the country.

After dinner Larry and Margaret were invited to the basement where they watched a YWAM video and met more guests. Two exchange students were going from Spain to Texas; another Swedish family was on their way to Morocco.

July 14, 1992

Larry did not get up for breakfast since he had not slept well. Margaret left him in bed and went on to breakfast, thinking that if he got on some sleep, he would be all right.

Margaret met the linguistics instructor and media coordinator for the North Africa network at breakfast. She lived at the center and had been away on holiday when they arrived. Margaret talked with the YWAM director and learned that there was a six hour delay at the Tangiers border because 1.5 million Moroccans are returning from Europe from holiday.

Margaret checked on Larry and found that he was suffering from a stomach disorder. She gave him plenty of liquids and he stayed in bed. Phillip, Kelly and Margaret walked to Torremolinos, some two miles away. They went to several travel agencies. One routed them to another section away from the regular ferry line to get a tour boat to Tangiers. The price was much higher, but without the long wait. They signed up for it to leave early Thursday morning. They came back to the center for dinner at 7:00. Larry tried to eat, but got sick again after dinner.

Margaret visited with the Venezuelan lady who shared her vision and her husband's vision for the city of Fes. He had seen a vision of angels and was given the message that God had many angels there at work and was sending more to reach the people. Margaret visited with the Swedish lady who told of her husband's conversion in Morocco as a YWAM team witnessed to him. Margaret went to bed with many thoughts swirling in her head.

Torremolinos—July 15, 1992

Larry was sick and got up several times during the night. He attempted to eat cereal and to drink tea for breakfast. All of the team got together to go to the Gospel Missionary Union Media Center in Malaga. They hitched a ride downtown with the YWAM director. He gave them a map for catching a bus. The bus they caught turned in the opposite direction and they had to take two more buses to get to Malaga.

They were amazed at the YWAM staff and their ingenuity in getting Bible correspondence courses into Morocco. They had a thirty-minute radio program produced via satellite into the country that advertising the courses. The courses were available to anyone who wrote and requested them. The mail does not seem to reach a lot of them. They depend on couriers to get the courses into the country. They have a young Arabic couple employed in their offices that grade the courses and prepare them for couriers to take back into the country.

Larry got sick in the middle of the tour and had to run to the bathroom. When he returned, he volunteered to be a courier for YWAM. The personnel got some large envelopes and stuffed them with items with the name of a man to call when they arrived in Meknes. Larry and Margaret paid for a taxi back to Torremolinos rather than taking the long bus ride in the heat with Larry's condition.

Larry and Margaret had lunch with the group at the center. They went to their room and rested after lunch. The Swedish couple had made arrangements to go as they did across on the boat to Tangiers. Since Larry was still not feeling well a nurse advised him to only drink mineral water in Spain. Margaret bought some mineral water before the trip.

Larry and Margaret returned to the center for dinner. After dinner the young Englishman, who is a worship leader, led the team in worship choruses with his guitar. This was a special time that concluded with prayer asking God's guidance as they attempted to tour Morocco.

Torremolinos—July 16, 1992

Larry and Margaret went to breakfast at 5:45 and joined the group at 6:30 to walk down the villa to the bus stop. Some held flashlights along the treacherous path as all eight of members of the team plugged along with their luggage. They arrived at the La Collina bus stop just as the bus arrived at 6:50. The bus took them to the boat which departed at 8:00. The boat ride across the Mediterranean was rough. They took Dramamine tablets. There must have been four or five hundred people on the boat. Many were European tourists on holiday.

The team arrived at the Tangiers port and was taken by a tour bus to the city. Margaret was drowsy from the Dramamine tablet and dozed through much of what the guide said. The tour bus stopped and let them off to go through the medina, which is a series of shops and attractions among the apartment houses. There were all sorts of bad smells. The sewer was over flowing and sewage waste flowed in the path where they walked. There was a snake charmer with live cobras that she passed around to tourists. Two Berber women walked up to Margaret as she stood away from the snakes. Both smiled and shook their heads, communicating to her that they too disliked snakes. The tour continued on to the carpet store, the leather shop and various other craft stores. The bus stopped at a restaurant for lunch. Larry and Philip hurried out to change some money before the banks closed at 2:00. They ended up at different banks somehow. Philip came back to join the group thinking that Larry would have come back. Larry was not there and Philip went to search for him. Their lunch was a beef or goat dish with couscous, almond filled cookies and mint tea.

Larry and Margaret left the group after lunch to catch a train to Meknes. The Swedish couple walked with them to the train station to say goodbye. They were to remain in Tangiers for another night. There were six Moroccans in the coach with Larry and Margaret. Fortunately, one of them spoke English and interpreted for the others. Larry and Margaret talked to the Moroccans during the entire 2.5 hour train ride. Larry became thirsty and got out his cup filling it with water from his bottle. They saw him drink from the plastic cup and each of them wanted to drink from his cup. He filled the cup and passed it to each of them. The English speaking girl told Larry and Margaret that she was an economics teacher in Casablanca. She became interested in Larry's bill cap and Margaret's straw hat. She tried both of them and Margaret got out her camera and took pictures of her wearing their hats. The Berber woman pointed to her veil and kept saying, "No. Islam." Margaret indicated that she understood. When she saw Margaret talking pictures of the others and promising to send them copies she asked the English-speaking girl to take some pictures of Margaret with her.

Larry and Margaret changed trains at 9:30. They were in a coach with a Moroccan girl and her father. They were traveling to Meknes for her to take her law examination. She said that she was not interested in being a lawyer, but was choosing this profession to please her father. She spoke English fluently but he did not speak any English. He owned a milk company south or Marrakesh. She invited Larry and Margaret to come to see them before they left Morocco. When they parted at the train station she kissed them on both cheeks saying, "Welcome to Morocco."

Philip and Kelly had met a French-speaking man from Casablanca. He agreed to be their guide for a tour of Meknes the next day. He had come to visit his parents in Meknes. Philip spoke French and was able to converse with him and to interpret for the team. They arrived in Meknes at 10:00 p.m. The French speaking man took them to their hotel. They ended up going to four hotels before finding rooms for the night. There was no air conditioning and the rooms were very hot. They did not sleep much and Larry got sick again that night.

Meknes—July 17, 1992[4]

Larry was not able to get up. When Phil came to the door, Margaret told him that they would stay in while the rest of them went on the tour. They got a late breakfast. Larry tried to drink some juice and got sick again. He was able to drink mineral water. He insisted that Margaret go on with the group while he stayed in the room to sleep. She went ahead with the group. The guide was one hour late. When he came he gave them a good tour, walking at least three miles and pointing out interesting parts of the city. The medina was most interesting. There were live chickens. The customer chooses a chicken and it is killed and feathered on the spot and given to the customer. The butcher, a devout Muslim would not allow Margaret to take photographs. The guide took the group to a large park area where the swimming pool was filled with youngsters. He showed them the school and the prison. The heat was really getting to them by then and he called a taxi to take them back to a restaurant in town. He helped them to order lunch. They had *tagine* (lamb cooked with sweet potatoes and covered with French fries and olives). It was a most delicious dish. They also had Moroccan bread.

The team returned to the hotel. Larry was still sick. Philip went to the telephone to call the contact man to pick up the Bible courses. He came to the room and volunteered to go to a local pharmacy to find some medication for Larry. Larry took the medication, but it did not seem to help. Philip called the person with the Bibles and asked him if he could contact a doctor. He called his doctor and got Larry an appointment for 9:00 the next morning. The team came in and prayed with him. He was up most of the night.

Meknes—July 18, 1992

Larry and Margaret got up at 6:30. The water had not been turned on yet. The city would cut the water off each night at 11:00 and it was not turned back on until about 8:00 in the morning. Larry was very weak and it took him a long time to get ready. The gentleman came with the Bibles. He is an English teacher and this was his cover in Morocco. He took Larry and Margaret to the doctor and the doctor took them directly into his office in spite of the fact that the waiting room was full of patients. He examined Larry and told him that he had an intestinal infection. He prescribed three medications and advised him not to eat anything but to drink plenty of liquids. He also advised him to stay in Meknes two more days to recover. He looked at Margaret and said, "He needs to rest." He told Larry that he had the same problem when he had visited Los Angeles recently. He seemed to have great sympathy. He only charged $10.00 for the office visit and the medication was only $8.00. He gave Larry and Margaret his home phone number and asked them to call him on Sunday or Monday if they needed him.

Their English teacher friend drove them back to the hotel. He told Larry and Margaret that there were not air conditioned hotels in the city. He offered to take them home with him for Larry to recover. Philip went to the pharmacy to have Larry's prescriptions filled while Larry and Margaret packed and checked out of the hotel. They were praising the Lord the whole time for his marvelous provisions. This kind man took them and also invited Philip and Kelly to come to his home. He and Philip went out and purchased chicken, potatoes, bread, and a melon. Larry rested in the cool room and they ate their first Moroccan style meal on sofas around the round table. Larry rested in this home atmosphere taking plenty of liquids with his medications. Margaret stayed with Larry that evening and their friend took Philip and Kelly to meet some Moroccan friends. After they returned two Moroccan friends dropped in to visit. One was the language center director in Meknes and the other made plastic optical lens as his cover.

Larry and Margaret agreed that Philip and Kelly should join the rest of the team for the tour in Marrakesh while Larry and Margaret remained in Meknes until Monday. They arranged to meet up with the group in Fes on Tuesday.

Meknes—July 19, 1992

Margaret encouraged Larry to eat a few spoons full of rice. Their English teacher friend taught a worship service with the Moroccans. He was teaching them from the Book of Revelation. He left for this service about 10:00. Larry slept most of the day. Margaret awakened him to eat more rice and drink more liquids every two hours. By noon he was able to eat a boiled egg. They had a worship time reading from Isaiah and praying. At all times through this the Holy Spirit impressed them to praise.

Their friend returned at 2:00. He wanted to take them out to eat. Margaret assured him that they were fine and would go out later to get water. Margaret insisted that he relax. She read a book from his library, *High Call, High Privilege* by Gail MacDonald. Philip called at 8:30 from Marrakesh to check on Larry. The trip down took them ten hours on a bus that was hot and not air conditioned. They were all hot and tired. Philip promised to call the following night to check on Larry.

Meknes—July 20, 1992

Larry was able to eat oatmeal for breakfast. Their host and Larry made plans. Larry would rest another day in Meknes and they would ride with him on Tuesday to Fes as he drove down to take his Arabic class at the language center there. He went out on an errand after breakfast. He returned and told Larry and Margaret that the neighbor had invited them over for lunch and that she would have Jell-O for Larry.

He drove them to the bank to change their money. He also went by the police station for him to pick up his residency form. The bank was a large beautiful building with air conditioning. It took some doing for their host to interpret Arabic to get their money with their Visa card. After seeing many people, the right person came to the desk and completed the transaction.

Their host then took them to an indoor coffee house on the way. They sat under huge ficas trees providing lots of shade during the hottest part of the day. Their host observed that most of the customers at this coffee shop were professional people. They drank citrus drinks and journeyed back to the street and over to the neighbor's house for lunch. The neighbor is the director of the language center and his wife grew up in Morocco as her parents were missionaries there. They have two small sons. She had fixed a lovely tagine in the center of a round table by the couches. She ushered them in and seated them, asked the blessing then broke the bread and passed it around the table. She demonstrated how they pinch off a small portion of the bread and scoop up tagine from the community platter in the center of the table. The tagine consisted of tiny meatballs, green beans and onions and was cooked in tomato sauce. It was most delicious. The director mentioned that his mother was from Monroe County, West Virginia so Larry and Margaret exchanged West Virginia stories.

The director's wife could speak fluent Arabic, having grown up in the country. She was interested that Larry and Margaret should come to Morocco to minister. She said that they could show proof of their retirement income and that there would be no problem with setting up residency. As they started to leave, she invited them to go with her to a Moroccan home after 6:00. Margaret was excited at the opportunity to meet some Moroccans and agreed to go while Larry went back to rest.

The director's wife came and walked with Margaret to the taxi stand to go downtown. When they arrived at the friend's apartment they found her ill with strep throat. She was afraid for them to come in because of her illness. She was a nurse. They then went to the language center where evening classes were in progress. The Spanish teacher was one of our kind. Margaret learned that the other missionaries used the expression, "one of our kind" to indicate other Christians. Leaving the language center they went to the square to view the lighted fountains. Many people were walking around, sitting and chatting on the benches. Others were taking photographs. Children were running and playing games. The city was cleaning buildings and fountains, and turning on the water because the king was coming to visit.

They said goodbye and Margaret expressed her thanks for such an enjoyable time as she stepped across the street to her host's home. Larry and Margaret walked a short distance down the street to get some water to take the next day. Larry was very tired after the walk.

Meknes to Fes—July 21, 1992

Larry slept fitfully and ran a high fever during the night. Larry and Margaret got up at 5:20 and had a light breakfast and got their luggage ready to leave with their host at 6:30. The drive took one hour. Their host took them to the language center in Fes. It is larger than the one in Meknes. One classroom is very ornate. It was possibly used as a Jewish synagogue in earlier years. Larry and Margaret then went to see a tour guide. He promised to come to see them at the hotel and give them a tour of the city.

They began to search for a hotel. The one beside the train station was full. Their host took them to a hotel a few blocks away (The Hotel Splendid). It had air conditioning and was the same price as the one in Meknes. Their host hugged them and said goodbye and he left for his class. Larry and Margaret took a short nap in their nice, cool room. They got up and went to a restaurant. Margaret got out her French menu and prayed, "We thank You Lord for the English-speaking person You are going to send to help us to order lunch." They looked up and their Meknes host was coming through the door. He had just finished his class and decided that he would stop by this restaurant for lunch before going back home. Larry and Margaret both exclaimed excitedly, "We just thanked the Lord for the English speaking person that He was sending us to help order lunch." He smiled and ushered them off around the corner to a French restaurant that served wonderful cheese omelets.

They had a lovely time chatting and he promised that he would bring his family to visit them in Virginia some time. He shared with them that his wife had been diagnosed with breast cancer and asked them to pray for her. They shall never forget this dear friend or their wonderful Lord who made all of this possible.

They returned to the room and rested until 4:00. They met the tour guide at 7:00 in the hotel lobby. He had brought the guide for the next day, a young man named Hafid. Larry and Margaret agreed to meet him at 9:30 the next morning. He walked with them to the bookstore. Philip called from the train station. They had contacted their Meknes friend and found out about their hotel. They came by to check on Larry and Margaret and visited for a few minutes.

Fes—July 22, 1992[5]

Larry rested well the night before and was up by 6:00. They went down to breakfast. The guide met them on schedule. They got a taxi and went to the Medina. What an experience! The tour took four hours with constant walking after the taxi let them out at the entrance. There were craftsmen of all kinds: wood work, brass work, grain mills, leather and dyeing, shoe cobblers, textiles, tailors, embroidery, weaving and shops for buying vegetables and fruits. Each of them purchased one piece of Moroccan clothing.

Larry and Margaret returned to the hotel and went to their evening meal. They decided to rest after they ate and then to go to the English bookstore to purchase maps of the area. Larry and Margaret then returned to the hotel to pack for the next morning.

Philip and Kelly went out to eat. Margaret went to get water and to go to the pharmacy to get eye drops for Larry. His eyes were beginning to look infected and swollen. Margaret found an English-speaking pharmacist and he brought some eye drops and instructed her to put them in six times a day. Margaret returned to the hotel just as Larry was leaving to meet the guide in the lobby to plan for Thursday's tour. Philip and Kelly returned and they all had prayer together.

Fes—July 23, 1992

Larry slept until 7:30. Larry and Margaret read the Bible and meditated before going down to breakfast at 9:30. After breakfast the guide met them and took a taxi to tour the countryside around Fes. They went high up on a mountain by an ancient fort where they were able to get interesting pictures of the medina and surrounding hillsides. The guide talked to them about the hard life in Morocco. His friend with him told of dropping out of the university as there was no hope for a job for university graduates. He wished to come to America, but had no hope of getting a visa. The Moroccan government does not want any of its people to leave.

They drove on to tour the pottery place. What an interesting place to see all of the skilled craftsmen at work with their clay at the potter's wheel and the young men painting intricate designs on their creations before baking them in the kilns. What an amazement to see very young boys skilled in painting such tiny, intricate designs. The guide told them that they only went to school long enough to read and write a little and then entered the factory to learn a trade.

Their taxi took Larry and Margaret from the pottery to the mineral springs. This is a large spring bubbling up with multitudes of people all around filling water jars and drinking from cups and bottles. They were trying to entice Larry and Margaret to drink. It was noon and very hot. Older people were putting their entire heads under the pipe flowing with the cold water. One father filled a water bottle and poured it over his little child as she gasped.

Walking from the springs Larry and Margaret went down several flights of winding stairs to the area below. There was a swimming pool completely filled with people. Some were camping under bedspread canopies. They were told that this area is a weekend spot in Fes. The medina closes on Friday and everyone rushes to this spot for rest and relaxation.

They completed their walk by stopping in the air conditioned hotel in the area for some iced lemon tea. They returned to the hotel and rested until they went to dinner. Larry had veal with mushrooms and vegetables. He cleaned his plate for the first time since his illness. Margaret had Moroccan couscous. They went back to the room and rested for about an hour before going to the English-speaking church.

They encountered a ten-year-old boy on their way to the church who insisted on being their guide. They finally crossed the street to avoid him. He rushed out in the traffic to catch up with them. When Larry and Margaret arrived at the church they rang the bell at the gate. The minister came and invited them in to meet some visitors from Tangiers. The minister's wife was very cordial. They learned that the minister was a retired navy chaplain. He had spent several years in Norfolk, Virginia. He shared with them that his daughter and her husband were members of a church in Texas.

Fes—July 24, 1992

Larry and Margaret awoke at 7:00 to the sound of birds, traffic and Arabic-speaking people in the streets below their hotel window. African young men, whether official guides or not, linger by the hotel lobby entrance to catch a tourist as they come in or watch guests coming down for breakfast to nab them. It is impossible to go on any streets without being approached by several guides.

Larry and Margaret went to the hotel restaurant for a late breakfast at 10:00. They needed to find another hotel since this one had no vacancies for that night. Larry found an English-speaking girl at the pharmacy and she told him about a hotel a few blocks from the Hotel Splendid. Larry came back and helped Margaret to get their luggage down to the lobby and to check out right at 12:00. He was totally winded after his illness and had to sit down before they could make the move. They went out to get a taxi and discovered that it was their holy day and that taxis were more busy than usual. They finally got a taxi and the drivers charged them 40 DHs, which was twice the regular rate. Their room had air conditioning.

Larry and Margaret rested until 4:00 and left the room to look for a restaurant. They decided to check the train station schedule. They got their directions confused and walked for over two hours. Finally they came to an affluent neighborhood where hired men were sweeping the streets and soldiers were stationed at each corner. They wondered why there was so much security. Finally they found the train station just as soldiers and policemen were clearing out the station. All passengers had to come to the park across from the station and wait. Larry and Margaret found a park bench and sat down. The soldiers spread about a dozen expensive royal red Moroccan carpets down the pavement in front of the train station entrance. Larry and Margaret assumed that the king must be arriving. No one in the crowd around them spoke English. Larry and Margaret were at a loss to know what was happening. Margaret sneaked her camera out of her purse and shot some pictures of the carpets and the police motorcades with motorcycles, cars and limousines with dignitaries. Later when the king's train arrived the security became tighter. One guard motioned for Margaret not to take pictures. She put her camera away. There was no fanfare—only some handshaking among the dignitaries with a kiss on each cheek. One siren sounded and the entourage was on its way. The red carpets were quickly rolled up and placed on trucks. The crowd dispersed and there business continued as usual. Larry and Margaret walked back to the hotel very tired after walking about five miles. They rested a while before going to dinner. They went down to the hotel restaurant. They took the French menus and could decipher omelets and yogurt. They ordered the cheese omelets which came with the hard French bread. The waiter spoke some English. Margaret asked him if he was aware that the king had come to Fes today. He did not seem impressed.

Fes—July 25, 1992

Larry and Margaret went to breakfast and came back to hotel to check out. The hotel personnel were helpful in giving Larry and Margaret maps and pointing out places of interest that they should see in

Rabat. Margaret waited with the luggage while Larry got a taxi. The train station was loaded. Margaret stood to the side at one bare spot with the luggage while Larry went to the ticket window. The ticket agent took about thirty minutes to get the tickets. While Margaret was standing with the luggage in the crowded area, Hafid, their guide for the past two days, spotted her and came over to talk. The train came in about that time. The train had air conditioning.

Near departure time a young Arab man joined them and later a young Arab woman in jeans. Both could speak French. Philip joined Larry and Margaret and was able to speak French with them. They passed some farming areas and Phil and Larry began to talk about farming and preserving food. Margaret pulled some snacks from her bag to share with their visitors. The girl remarked that one of the whole wheat crackers was delicious. She knew that much English. She stood up to get off at the next station and told them all goodbye. A well-dressed young Arab woman in western clothing joined them at this station. She spoke French and enjoyed conversation about farming remarking that the farms in America were much nicer than theirs. Soon the conversation turned to ask Larry and Margaret what meats they ate in America. They told them that they mostly ate chicken, beef and fish. They were appalled that they seldom ate lamb. They wanted to share with Larry and Margaret about the big feast when each family kills a lamb and sometimes two in commemoration of Abraham's offering a sheep instead of Ishmael.

They insisted that the son that Abraham was going to offer was Ishmael. Then they asked what religion Larry and Margaret professed and what feasts they celebrated. Philip explained that they were Christians and told them about Thanksgiving and Christmas feasts. Larry prodded Philip to tell them about Easter. They immediately asked him, "Who is Jesus Christ?" Philip elaborated that Jesus Christ was our savior. They insisted that Jesus, whom they call *Isa*, is only a good prophet.

The lady got up to leave at the next station. Her friend remained with Larry and wanted to take them to a cafe for cold drinks and offered to help them find a hotel. Not too far from the train station they found a large outdoor café under the ficas trees. This was the first time that they had seen women and children seated at outdoor cafes. Rabat is more western than the other cities they had visited. Their friend ordered their drinks. As they visited Larry asked Philip to ask him if his parents were still living. "Oh yes," he replied. "My mother lives here in Rabat and my father lives in Fes." He was returning from visiting his father. He remarked, "My father has many wives." Philip asked him how many and he responded, "79." Phil exclaimed, "He must be very rich to support that many wives!" "Yes," he said smiling. Then he suggested to Philip that Larry and Margaret should wait at the table with the luggage while he and Philip located a hotel.

The heavy ficas trees turned out to be the roosting place for a multitude of birds. Larry and Margaret decided to move when one bird blessed Margaret with a fresh wet dropping right on her skirt. By the time Philip and their friend returned, Margaret told them that they might have to shovel them out. Larry and Margaret went to another Hotel Splendid just a few blocks away. Their room had a shower and a sink. They shared a commode down the hall with four other rooms.

Rabat was the quietest city that they visited on Saturday night. The weather was cooler and conducive to sleep. The humidity was higher in Rabat than on the Atlantic coast. They went to a restaurant across the street to eat a light meal and to purchase mineral water for the next day. Philip took a walk to search for an English-speaking church.

Rabat—July 26, 1992[6]

Larry woke up early and felt like taking a walk while Margaret got ready. Philip came to tell them that he had found the church and that the English service was at 11:00. They walked about six blocks and stopped to get a pastry and English tea and arrived at the church just in time. Piano music sounded a prelude. They were warmly greeted by the associate pastor and then by the pastor. The associate pastor's wife led the singing. Songs were all related to heaven. A variety had been chosen to accommodate all types of Protestants. The children went up front for a children's sermon about heaven. After more music, a young man read the scripture from Philippians 3. The minister then preached on our citizenship not being here. He focused on drawing closer to Christ that we might learn who we are in Christ. In learning to know Him we learn who we are. He emphasized forgetting about the past.

At the end of the service everyone was invited to go to the pastor's home for a pot luck dinner. He invited Larry and Margaret to come. The pastor's wife volunteered to take them in her car. They insisted on getting bread at a bakery that they spotted across from their home. The traffic was not quite as hectic here as in other Moroccan cities. The families from the church began coming in with food, real American food (salads, vegetables and fruits, macaroni, desserts and chicken). They had not had salads since entering Morocco. They ate lots of carrots.

Many of the families from the church work for the embassy. There was one university professor from the University of Missouri that was sponsored by the government to teach Moroccans. He teaches veterinary science courses at the University in Rabat. He and his wife drive a new car, the first Larry and Margaret had seen in Morocco. Larry enjoyed talking with him about his castor bean research. He thought that it was highly feasible. He indicated that he would be in the states in September and gave Larry a contact number.

Philip talked to many people, one a converted Muslim who had returned from the states before completing his education because his money was depleted. He was living with his family and looking for a job. Everywhere they went there were always young men who would approach them about coming to the states. A young student that had just returned from working at a youth camp in the High Atlas Mountains and was interested in getting the names of universities in America that offered accounting courses stopped to talk with them.

Margaret learned from the pastor's wife that there was an American school in Rabat that would like to hire American teachers. They expressed their appreciation to the pastor and his wife as they were leaving and the university professor graciously offered to drive them to their hotel in his new car.

Larry and Margaret rested in their rooms until 7:00 and their young Arab friend, Taid, returned to take them on a tour or Rabat's medina. He purchased some delicious Moroccan pastry for them on the way to the medina. They walked through the medina, which was much cleaner than other cities they had visited. There were beggars every few feet, women with children on their laps sitting on the pavement. Taid informed them that begging was a way of life for these women. If they did not have children they would hire children to sit with them to beg.

After visiting the medina, they went down to see the Atlantic Ocean. There is a huge fort near the ocean and outside it a large Arab graveyard. Arab soldiers who were killed outside the fort were buried here. They returned through the medina stopping off at a sidewalk café for Moroccan soup.

Rabat—July 27, 1992

Larry and Margaret were awakened at 4:45. They were both nauseous. They thought that the Moroccan soup must have made them sick. Philip came to their room about 9:00 and they discussed plans for going to Tangiers the next day. They decided to go to the bank to exchange money for the trip. When they got to the automatic teller across the street, they could not get their Visa card to function. Larry had to stand in a long line at the bank to exchange traveler's checks while Philip and Margaret went to find pastries and mineral water for breakfast. Larry ended up waiting an hour and a half.

They walked to the Muse Lee Mohammed V monument and took some pictures. The scene was beautiful overlooking the Atlantic into the city of Salé. After visiting the Muse Lee Mohammed V they walked to where they could hail a taxi to see the king's palace. They then asked the driver to take them to the

Roman ruins at Chillah. Here they saw a spring where there were large black eels the size of snakes living in the water. Women come there and fed the eels boiled eggs and poured water from the spring over their heads and pray to have children. The spring is supposed to bring fertility. A young man was asking for donations in order to explain about the eels and fertility rites. Leaving these ruins Larry and Margaret walked almost all the way back into town before they could get a taxi. It was near closing time for the shops. They finally got a taxi to take them to the gardens near the Atlantic.

They arrived at the walled kibosh that housed the gardens. They had scarcely gotten in when a young man imposed himself on them as their guide. They assured him that they did not need a guide and did not want one. He then told them that he was a student and would just walk along with them. They could not shake him. Many people live in the kibosh. Many doors have door knockers of Fatima's hand which is supposed to signify good luck. As they wound their way to the top they had an excellent view of the Atlantic where Moroccans of all descriptions were moving like ants on the beach and swimming in the ocean. Leaving this scene they wound their way back down to the street. Their tag along guide approached them for money. They assured him that they had not hired him and they left him delivering favored Arab curses. At this point, they were so tired that they felt that they did not want to see anything else in Rabat except their hotel room. They rested in their room for a few minutes before going to dinner. After dinner, their young Arab friend came bounding up the steps wanting to take them out again. Larry and Margaret explained that they had just eaten and did not feel like going out.

Rabat- July 28, 1992

Larry and Margaret dressed and packed and then went to the restaurant down the street for tea and a sweet roll. They ordered English tea and they brought a cup of boiling milk and a tea bag. Larry and Margaret returned to the hotel after breakfast, checked out and walked to the train station a few blocks away. They caught the train at 8:15. As usual there was a mad stampede to get to the door. They had to stand in the hall for a few moments before two seats became available. Philip found a seat in another cab. Some people stood for the entire five-hour trip to Tangiers. One young Moroccan in Larry and Margaret's cab spoke English and carried on a conversation with those around her. This young man was an accounting student at Stanford University. His father worked for the king.

An older man with sores on his foot was seated near the student and asked him if Americans had a cure for diabetes. Larry and Margaret informed him that diabetes was controlled by diet, or sometimes medication or insulin in their country. Larry noted that he had just drunk a can of Pepsi. Larry told him that the Pepsi was loaded with sugar. He got out his kit to show him that he had checked his blood and that his sugar was low. His concept of cleanliness was poor. He was not wearing socks or covering the sores on his foot with a bandage. He sifted snuff and stuffed it up his nostrils. The remainder he dusted on the sores on his foot. When the train reached Tangiers he took his cane and demanded a young Moroccan to help with his bags and was out of the train and on the ferry before Larry and Margaret.

As Larry and Margaret hustled in the line to have their passports checked, a young Dutch girl who was a student traveling alone started up a conversation with them. The ferry was to leave in thirty minutes and they were near the end of a long line. She remarked that it was important that she make this ferry so that she could meet her train in Algeciras headed for France. Finally another line opened up and the crowd was rushed to the ferry. After leaving their luggage with the baggage clerk, they walked over to the huge ferry and located a restroom and cafeteria. Larry and Margaret stopped at one of the tables and sat down to drink their mineral water. The air conditioning had gone out on the train for about an hour and they were hot. They then walked up on the upper deck to take photographs. They watched a big ship being directed into the harbor by a pilot ship from Beirut. They returned to the lower level and noted that seats and tables had filled and they had to search for a seat. They finally saw a lone girl reading at a table and asked if they might join her. When she looked up and saw that they were her English-speaking friends she cordially welcomed them to join her. She explained that she had felt insecure about traveling alone. Larry and Margaret asked the young student to join them as they went to the cafeteria. They got chicken with vegetables.

Larry and Margaret walked through customs and walked about three blocks to the bus station. As they bought their tickets they barely had time to get on the bus before it departed. They rode the bus for 2.5 hours seeing the beautiful cities and countryside. They arrived in Torremolinos at 11:15. A taxi pulled in just as the bus did and they went straight to the YWAM guest house. They had been traveling for 18 hours. The YWAM staff greeted them warmly and showed them to their rooms. They offered them food and a cup of tea, but Larry and Margaret declined so that they could get their rest. As they showed them to their rooms, they brought tea bags, a hot pot of cream and fresh roses in bud vases from the garden.

Torremolinos—July 29, 1992

Larry and Margaret had a good night of rest. Margaret noticed that her left leg was stiff and tired when she got up. She thought that this was from Monday's walking and the 18 hours that she had spent traveling in cramped conditions. Larry and Margaret met everyone for toast and tea. The linguistics and networking coordinator came to see if they had everything that they needed.

After breakfast, Margaret fell on the four-inch step from the bathroom and hurt her right foot and right elbow. They went to the YWAM library until lunch. They enjoyed the rice, egg and vegetable dish with watermelon for dessert that the staff prepared. The king's kids told them that they were performing in the city square that night and invited them to come and hear them. After their siesta time from 3:00 to 5:00 they could hear them practicing for their performance. They were ushered into the dining area for sandwiches before the performance. There was a crowd sitting on the park benches and the folding seats that the city had placed for the audience. The kids gave a lively performance of songs, testimonies and dancing. They were well received. Larry and Margaret returned to the center after the performance and went on to their room to rest.

Torremolinos—July 30, 1992

Larry and Margaret got up and Larry walked two miles to town to get money changed to buy mineral water and juice. At lunch they visited with the king's kids and their sponsors. They invited Larry and Margaret to come downstairs for the fun time which was to be after dinner. Their team spent most of the afternoon reading research reports from the YWAM library and discussing the North African ministry as they sat on the back veranda overlooking the Mediterranean.

Larry and Margaret joined Pastor Bob and his wife from the Evangelical Community Church in Torremolinos for dinner. After dinner, they joined the king's kids in the basement for their skits, mimes, games and other stunts until 10:00. Their group included all nationalities laughing and enjoying themselves. The group had a short time of sharing on the veranda before they went to their rooms to rest for the evening.

July 31, 1992

Larry and Margaret met a couple in the dining room with their baby that had come in from Brussels the previous night. He is Egyptian and she is German. They pastor a church in Brussels which has an outreach ministry to the Muslims. They had recently had a children's crusade which drew many Muslim children. At the conclusion they had a dinner inviting the children's parents. Fifteen parents came. This was an excellent response for Muslims.

Larry and Margaret had a conference with the YWAM linguistic and networking coordinator before lunch. She gave them a projected schedule for language school in Arabic for the next year. The YWAM director's wife helped Larry, Margaret and Philip to load their luggage in their old Land Rover to drive them to Malaga to the airport. She weaved in and out of traffic like one of the Muslims. They kissed her on both cheeks and waved goodbye, as Larry paid her what would have been their taxi fee.

Larry and Margaret had confirmed seats in the non-smoking section on the plane. They were told that these seats had been taken. There were gorgeous, well-manicured lawns as they landed in Belgium. This was in stark contrast to the dry conditions that they had seen in dry countries for the last three weeks where water was at a premium. They got a shuttle to the Hotel Novotel. The rooms were very comfortable. They went down to the hotel restaurant to get a snack before going to bed.

Brussels, Belgium—August 1, 1992

Larry and Margaret spent some quiet time with the Lord in praise for the trip that He had helped them to accomplish. Larry and Margaret met Philip for a buffet breakfast in the hotel restaurant. Several English-speaking people were there from Britain. Margaret shopped at a few of the shops in the hotel before they were to catch their plane. The terminal was very hot. When they got to the lower level the air was on slightly. This time they were given center aisle seats where they would have plenty of leg room for the 7.5 hour flight.

When the plane landed in Boston at 2:30 p.m., Larry and Margaret were happy to see the American flag and the *Welcome to the United States* sign. Many of the customs personnel welcomed them home. After a brief layover in Boston they boarded their flight for Norfolk, Virginia. They arrived at 8:30 and were greeted by Philip's friend who took Larry to pick up their car. When he returned they loaded the luggage in the back and drove to the White's home on Indian River to pick up Larry and Margaret's computer and typewriter. Joyce White greeted them warmly and insisted that they spend the night rather than driving in search of a motel. Larry and Margaret did not have to be persuaded as they were quite tired. The Whites were such a gracious couple. Larry and Margaret had stayed with them for three weeks while they were in training at Regent University. God is so good!

When Larry and Margaret got back to Dublin, Virginia they began to reflect back over their trip and to realize the many ways in which God wrought miracles for them. They remembered these experiences and trusted God to lead them and to provide for their needs as they continued on the journey.

Prayer and Outreach Focus

Pray for the missionaries in the North African region. They are ministering to a diverse group of people (French, Spanish, Berbers and many others). They are struggling to learn the languages that are necessary to communicate with these individuals. They cannot speak openly about the scriptures. Pray for guidance and protection as they witness.

Chapter Twelve

The Covering

He who dwells in the shelter of the Most High will rest in the shadow of the Almighty (Psalm 91:1).

Jesse and Mabel Bishop would have been proud of their brood. By 1993, they numbered over thirty people. They were all engaged in some sort of Christian service. Prayer was as important to the Bishop offspring as it had been for Jesse and Mabel. Jim Bishop invited the entire family to his home in Greensboro, North Carolina for New Year's Day. It was not uncommon for the Bishop family to get together, but this gathering was going to be different.

January 1, 1993 would mark the beginning of a new era for the Bishop family especially for Larry and Margaret. They were to leave a few days later for Morocco. We all knew many of the challenges and dangers that they would face. We knew that the Arabic language would be difficult for them to learn especially at their ages. We knew that there was political unrest and that Americans particularly Christians were not welcome on foreign soil. We had heard reports of Christians being tortured, beaten and imprisoned for their faith.

We recognized as we never had before that Larry and Margaret would need the covering of the blood of Jesus in order for their mission to be successful and in order for them to return home safely. We all loved them dearly and this parting was a painful one for all of us. We recognized more than ever that we must trust God for their protection. We enjoyed feasting on Christmas treats for three days before New Year's and visiting with the family. We all seemed to avoid talking about Larry and Margaret leaving. It would not be the same to not have Larry to sing the "Twelve Days of Christmas" during our family gatherings or to have all of Margaret's scrumptious goodies.

On New Year's Day, Larry again shared the vision that the Lord had shared with him about the Berbers. We all gathered in a circle and each of us prayed a prayer for them. The prayer seemed to give us all peace. We all knew that whatever obstacles and problems that they would encounter that the Lord would be with them to deliver them and to uphold them by his strong right hand.

We all went back to our duties the next day as Larry and Margaret prepared to fly to Morocco. We knew that we would need to continue to plead the blood of Jesus over their lives each day while they were gone. The transfusion that Larry had been commanded to affect would not be an easy task. These were a people bent on self-destruction as Larry had been told. They saw Christ as a stumbling block and not a corner stone. They did not want to be transfused with the blood of Jesus. They did not believe that the blood of Jesus could atone for their sins. Jesus was only a good prophet as far as they were concerned. They believed that they could earn their salvation through good works and moral living.

Margaret later told about many people that they witnessed to who accepted them as friends and treated them with respect, but would not accept Jesus as their savior because of their hardened hearts. She commented that one young man saw Jesus as a stumbling block and that he had vowed that he would die a Muslim. They worked with this young man for years. He loved and respected them, but he was always quick to let them know that he would not have anything to do with Jesus Christ.

Aileen wrote about a large group of ministers and friends who went to the airport in Roanoke, Virginia when Larry and Margaret left to pray for their safety and for their mission to be a successful one. Aileen must have been remembering the nights that she spent under the stars as a child with her dad when he talked about the stars and God's care for us when she remarked, "We can release them to the Lord's safe keeping as they are under the same sky, moon, stars and sun that God created for all of us. It is not his will for any to perish" (Letter to Marie Jan. 25, 1993).[1]

The first months that Larry and Margaret were in North Africa were extremely trying as they attempted to learn the language and the culture. They lived with another family and did not know where they would find housing since housing was in short supply. They dealt with the extremely cold temperatures and no heat or hot water in buildings. They had to walk most of the places that they went or at least walk some distance to a bus stop. They did not have a car for about the first eighteen months that they were in North Africa. Walking made them more vulnerable to robbers and to other dangers. They did not have a telephone until November, 1993 and email was not always available. Mail was often confiscated and read so they had to be careful not to mention anything about God or church in their letters. Everything had to be coded so that no one would be suspicious of their activity.

Family and friends could only pray and hope for the best. During this time, we would hear about missionaries who had been arrested quite frequently. Usually the names were not released at least in the beginning so we did not know whether Larry and Margaret were safe. We continued to trust and pray and would always send up a prayer of thanksgiving when we learned that they were safe.

Margaret wrote about many people who would contact them and tell them that they were praying for them every day. One little eight-year-old girl told Larry that every time she asked the blessing over her food she added, "Lord bless those missionaries!" These intercessory prayers were what helped Larry and Margaret to bear fruit in this closed country. Another major source of spiritual strength for Larry and Margaret was the English-speaking church that they found. They became involved in the church and Larry filled in as pastor when they did not have a full time pastor.

There were times when they went through unpleasant things, but the Lord gave them the grace to endure and His peace. They were robbed, their car was stolen and they dealt with angry Muslims who did not understand or tolerate Christianity. Larry suffered with cancer and continued to pray and minister to the people that God sent across his path as long as he was physically able. Margaret had several falls and broken bones and dealt with the problems that she faced with macular degeneration. The problems were there, but God's grace was sufficient. The enemy roared like a lion at times, but the blood of Jesus Christ covered and protected them.

Margaret wrote about their language instructor who had suffered many beatings by the police. She wrote that he was being watched constantly to determine what activities he was engaged in, but his faith remained firm. "Some fall back when persecution becomes severe. We feel so humbled to be here in the presence of people who suffer so much and yet are so friendly and helpful to us. How much do we in the states take for granted of all the freedoms we enjoy?" (Email from Margaret 3-26-93) [2]

Larry and Margaret met a lady who became a close friend while they were there who had been a midwife for forty years in Morocco. She, too, had suffered many beatings and imprisonment for the cause of Christ.

Larry and Margaret were blessed with the prayers of people whom they had led to the Lord while they were in Morocco. Margaret wrote about a lady who lived in her neighborhood that was having migraine headaches and had become severely depressed. Her husband came to Margaret and invited her to come and pray with his wife. Margaret went into the darkened bedroom and began to talk with the woman. She had not been able to teach her classes in weeks. She was depending on two of her nieces to do all of her household chores. Margaret asked her if she could pray for her and she nodded affirmatively. Margaret laid her hand on the lady's forehead and prayed for healing 'in Jesus's name.' The lady thanked her and Margaret visited her each day to encourage her. The family was expecting her to die. By the third day, Margaret had her out walking in the bright sunlight and encouraged her to open shutters to let light in the apartment. On the fifth day, Margaret invited a doctor friend to go with her to examine the woman. The doctor advised her to discontinue the anti-depressants that the Moroccan doctor had prescribed. After the examination the three of them joined hands for prayer. Margaret prayed and then the doctor prayed. Then to their amazement, the lady closed the prayer by praying for them. The next few days the lady was able to go out and drive the car and do her own shopping and housework. God had performed a miracle!

Margaret told about this lady and her husband coming to visit them the night before they were to fly out to the United States to say goodbye. She had baked a plate of cookies for them to take on their trip and wanted to pray with them before they left.

Prayer and Outreach Focus

Missionaries need protection when they go to foreign countries, especially countries where Christians are considered to be infidels and where they are not permitted to openly teach and preach the Gospel message. There are many security issues that missionaries face in foreign countries that you will read about in the next chapters. Police officers often turn their heads when foreigners are robbed, mugged, or otherwise mistreated. Missionaries, like all of us need protection from spiritual forces that might discourage them in their walk or cause them to stumble so that they could not be effective witnesses. Pray for the blood of Jesus to provide a spiritual, emotional and physical covering for missionaries that you know.

Chapter Thirteen

Learning the Arabic Language
& Adapting to the Culture

. . . I have been all things to all men so that by all possible means I might save some. I do all this for the sake of the gospel that I may share in its blessings (I Corinthians 9:22-23).

Larry and Margaret arrived in Torremolinos, Spain (near Gibraltar) in January, 1993.[1] They first stayed at the Youth with a Mission (YWAM) center there. On February 3rd, they caught the ferry to Tangier, Morocco.[2] Even though Tangier is just across the strait of Gibraltar, it took 2.5 hours for the ferry to make the trip.

Margaret had learned from a previous trip to sit still and look straight ahead in order to avoid motion sickness. Larry and Margaret had learned to carry a snack as food was not available on the ferry and there were sometimes lengthy delays with loading the ferry. There were no delays in unloading the ferry. Young Moroccans were always available for hire to transport luggage. It was sometimes difficult to communicate with them where the luggage was to be taken before they disappeared into the crowd. On one occasion, some young boys took off to hail a taxi when they had planned to go to their next destination by train. They had to catch up with them and explain in their limited Arabic that the luggage was to be taken to the train station.

Cell phones with international plans were not generally available in 1993 and email was only available on a limited basis when one could find a place with electricity and Ethernet connections. Larry and Margaret had to locate a public telephone booth or communicate by fax or letter.

The train that they took to Fes, Morocco was quite dirty. They soon learned that most of the city was dirty with garbage spilling out in the streets. It became one of Larry's projects while he was in Fes to clean up the streets. Soon some of the Moroccans were following his example and trying to clean up the trash and garbage that had been strewn on the streets.

They first went to the Youth with a Mission Language Center (YWAM) where they learned that they would be placed in a home with a Moroccan family while they attended the language school to learn Arabic. Staying with this family gave them the opportunity to practice their language skills and to learn the culture. If you would like to try your Arabic, you can go to the Arabic translator.[3] When you click on this link, you will notice two boxes. Click "English" over the box on the left and type the word "water" in the white box. Click on the speaker button on the right side and you will hear the Arabic pronunciation for water. You will also see how water is written in Arabic.

Cold Buildings & Cold Water

Larry and Margaret were soon searching for blankets, hot water bottles and anything to keep them warm in the cold buildings in Fes. The building where they attended language class was not heated at all. Their first session started at 8:00 a.m. and the temperatures inside the building were as cold as the outdoors. They would attend their morning session, eat lunch at the center and then have an afternoon session. By the end of the day they would be chilled to the bone.

Most of the buildings are constructed of tile and have high ceilings. They were built centuries ago and were not insulated. The windows are not energy efficient. It is difficult to find caulking or any other insulating materials. Someone at the language center took pity on the students later the first week and installed a small propane heater in the room. They found a hot pot to make hot tea during their breaks. Most of the buildings did not have hot water. The family that Larry and Margaret lived with while they went to language school had a crude, homemade water heater on the roof that was heated with wood. The family had built a shed around the hot water heater and would go there to bathe once a week in a galvanized tub.

Banking & Security

Banking hours are not from 9 to 5 in Morocco. The Moroccans close the banks in the early afternoon. Tourists and foreigners have to learn the individual times that the banks are open in their area. Other businesses also shut down in the early afternoon. Tourists soon learn to never carry a wallet in a back pocket. Ladies should avoid carrying money, passports, or anything of value in their purses. Zippered pockets on the inside of jackets or wallets that can be worn under clothing are the best. It is practically impossible to board a bus, train, ferry, or even to walk down the crowded streets without encountering pickpockets. They have practiced their trade since early childhood and they are quite skilled. They can remove wallets, purses, jewelry and other valuables without the owner noticing in many cases. Larry and Margaret both had several incidents where things were stolen from them or when they had to fight off thieves.

Marrakech

Larry and Margaret were introduced to the Moroccan marketplace practices in the square as they passed through Marrakech (Morocco City) on their way to Fes. The Berber villagers sell their goods and provide entertainment for tourists. Tourists would circle each booth to purchase goods or to enjoy the entertainment. Marrakech is known as the Red City. It is so named for the natural red-ochre pigment in the paint on its walls and buildings.[4]

The Djemaa el Fna or the square is the heart of the activity. It is in the Djemaa el Fna that tourists gather around groups of acrobats, drummers, pipe musicians, dancers, storytellers and comedians. Other attractions in the area include the still basins of the Agdal and Menara gardens, the delicate Granada-style carving of the Saadian Tombs and the Koutoubia Minaret. The Koutoubia Minaret is considered by most to be the most perfect Islamic monument in North Africa.[5]

The ancient Medina with its fortified wall was founded by Sultan Youssef Ben Tachfine in the middle ages and the colonial Ville Nouvelle, built by the French in the mid-twentieth century. Larry and Margaret must have thought that they had taken a trip back in time to the days of the Apostle Paul as they toured the Medina for the first time. There was a lady snake charmer. She had young men playing the traditional Muslim music and at certain intervals she would stop them and address the people in an auctioneer tone, luring them to her booth. She put a boiled egg out for the cobra to crawl out and coil as he charmed people. Beggars were all around them in the Medina.

Karaouine Mosque

Larry and Margaret passed the Karaouine Mosque as they walked through the city. The Karaouine Mosque is the oldest mosque in the world and part of the oldest university, the University of Al-Karaouine. As many as 20,000 Muslims flock to the Karaouine Mosque to pray. It is the largest mosque in North Africa. Fatima Al-Fihri, Mohammed Al-Fihri's daughter who was a wealthy merchant in the 9th century donated some of the funds from her inheritance to build the Karaouine Mosque. The Karaouine Mosque has ornate tile, plasterwork, woodcarvings, paintings and courtyards that were typical of the Moroccan architecture of that era. [6]

They saw more local artisans at work near the mosque milling flour, sewing *kaftans* and *jellabas*, making wood furniture, shining the brass filigree pieces, turning pottery, making leather goods and jewelry. There were shoe cobblers and boys begging to shine shoes. Larry stopped for a shoe shine on their first visit.

The jellaba is a loose-fitting robe with a hood that the Moroccans wear over their clothes. The Moroccans wear wool jellabas in the winter much like Americans wear coats for warmth. Men usually just wear jellabas in the winter or for special occasions. Women wear them as a covering any time they are in public along with a scarf. The jellaba that women wear is usually a colorful fabric. Men's jellabas are usually in darker colors like men's suits in America. Men sometimes wear a red cap, called a fez or tarbouche,[7] and yellow leather slippers, known as baboush or belgha with their jellabas for special occasions.[8]

The kaftan is a long robe, but does not have a hood. The kaftan is made of more expensive fabrics such as silk and is worn for weddings and formal occasions. Women sometimes wear a kaftan when they receive important guests in their homes for a holiday.[9]

Jewelry

There are many varieties of Moroccan jewelry. The jewelry in the city is made by Jewish merchants with intricate gold details and precious stones. The Berber jewelry is made with silver and less costly stones such as coral and amber.[10]

Leather

The Moroccans are known for their soft leather products. Americans prize items such as Moroccan leather Bibles. Most of the Moroccans wear *babouches*. Babouches are flat-soled slippers. These are made of different colors of leather. Some of the babouches have designs embroidered on them and other embellishments. [11 and 12]

Moroccan Music

Moroccan music shows the many influences that make up the Moroccan people. Moroccan culture has been strongly influenced by the French, Spanish, English, the Berbers and various other African cultures. There is the Berber and Chaabi folk music, Classical, Gnawa and Sufi mystical music, and Malhun. Chaabi music has an English influence. Chaabi is considered pop music in Morocco and is what most street musicians play in the marketplace and for Moroccan festivals. Sufi music is part of the Sufi Muslim religious tradition and is intended to bring about a trance like state while members of the Sufi brotherhood pray or meditate. Malhun music consists of ballads written about working class people. Malhun is the Moroccan equivalent of country music. Rai is Moroccan rock music. [13-16]

Moroccan Cooking

The Mediterranean diet is taunted by the Mayo Clinic and by many health experts as being a healthy diet.[17] Individuals in the Mediterranean area are known to have lower cancer and heart disease rates, because they get plenty of exercise and follow a diet that is low in cholesterol and sugar. The Mediterranean diet includes lots of fresh fruits and vegetables, whole grains, olive oil, beans and nuts. Moroccans use herbs and spices to flavor food instead of salt or use very little salt. They eat moderate amounts of fish, poultry, eggs, yogurt and cheese and very little red meat. Moroccans and most people in the Middle East eat with family or friends. Some medical experts believe that eating with other people encourages a person to eat less and has other positive psychological benefits that are healthy. Moroccan foods have a beautiful presentation with lots of color since they include so many fruits and vegetables. The presentation also helps a person to have a perception of being satisfied.

Larry and Margaret enjoyed the Moroccan dishes, especially the fresh fruits and vegetables and the breads. Margaret learned to cook many of their dishes and would always have a table full of guests for Sunday dinner and many other times during the week. Larry and Margaret enjoyed cooking and eating many Moroccan dishes.[18]

Larry and Margaret learned to shop for fresh fruits and vegetables in the *souk* or market every day.[19] Margaret enjoyed the fresh buttermilk and other dairy products. She once told some of the Moroccans that it was her job to churn the buttermilk and butter when she was growing up. Larry told that it was his job to milk the cow. He told that one spout gave plain milk, another chocolate, one spout buttermilk and the other ice cream. It took quite a bit of interpreting for the Moroccans to understand his joke. Larry and Margaret soon learned that ice cream was a common word in any language. They would always have more people than they could manage when they announced that they would serve ice cream.

Fruits and Vegetables

Orange and lemon groves are plentiful in Morocco. Most other fruits and vegetables are readily available at the open markets. The main vegetable that Larry and Margaret missed while in Morocco was corn on the cob. Larry and Margaret soon learned that they needed to soak all fresh vegetables and fruits in a mild solution of Clorox water and then rinse in mineral water. Many Americans are following similar processes after recent outbreaks of E.coli and other bacterial diseases.

Moroccans often serve fresh oranges, dates and figs for desert.[22-23] Orange blossoms are sometimes used as a garnish on Moroccan dishes. Orange blossoms are also used in making fragrances that are sold in the market.[20] Lemons are plentiful in Morocco. One of the Moroccan specialties is preserved lemons.[21] Preserved lemons are used in couscous, tagine and many Moroccan recipes.

Moroccan Salads

Lots of vegetable and fruit salads are available in Morocco since they have an abundance of fresh vegetables and fruits. Vegetable salads or raw vegetables are sometimes served along the edges of the communal platter along with the couscous and tagine. [24]

Moroccan Pastilla or Bastilia (Pigeon Pie)

One of the first days in Fes, Larry and Margaret tried pigeon pie. Pigeon pie is a Moroccan specialty that is prepared much like chicken pot pie in America. [25]The pigeons are stewed, deboned and chopped. The pigeon is added to a pastry shell and cooked with vegetables, herbs and spices. The Moroccans eat pigeon pie with their fingers. They sometimes provide a bowl of powdered sugar to dip the pie in as it is eaten. Sometimes pigeon pie is served as an appetizer or for the afternoon tea. It is usually followed by a tagine.[26]

Moroccan Bread

Margaret told about observing their hostess making Moroccan bread. She measured out the flour in a large glazed pottery bowl and put it on the floor and folded a rug in front of it. She knelt on this rug and worked from there, pouring in warm water from the tea kettle with the yeast mixture and mixing it with her hands. She kneaded the bread for a long time, longer than we normally knead yeast bread in America. She then shaped it into small balls of dough and placed them on the table. She shaped them carefully and patted them flat. She covered the bread with a large table linen and then placed an afghan on top of that. There was no way that the bread would get a draft even in this cold house.

Margaret noticed that most of the ladies were taking their bread to a bakery in the old Medina to be baked in a public oven. She decided to try having the baker to bake her bread. She asked the baker if she could bring her bread and he smiled and shook his head affirmatively. She went back to her apartment and mixed her yeast dough letting it rise for one hour before forming it into pones like they bake it. She put four of them in two long pans, covered them with towels and took them to the baker. He looked under her towels and showed her that he would pat them down and pierce them with a fork. She returned in two hours to pick up her bread. The women came out on the terraces to watch her picking up her bread. They smiled and waved wildly at her indicating their approval that she had accepted their custom. One of them exclaimed, "Now you are truly Moroccan. You have made the mint tea and the hobes (bread) also."

The Moroccans also serve cornbread, more like corn fritters with olives. Most bread is served with fresh olives. One of the methods that Margaret used to teach the Moroccan ladies English was to teach them to read recipes and to let them bake things during their class. This helped to lighten things a bit and gave them something to take home to enjoy with their families.[27]

Couscous

Couscous is a main staple in Morocco. Couscous is not grown like rice. It is made from semolina wheat that is formed in to small granules that are smaller than rice. Couscous is very similar to rice and is served with stewed vegetables and meat. Moroccan meals are served on a large platter in the center of the table. Guests are each given a spoon and eat directly from the common platter or eat with their hands. Couscous can be purchased in grocery stores in America.[28]

Tagine

Tagine is a Moroccan stew. It is named after the tagine pot in which it is prepared. The tagine pot is a cone-shaped terra cotta pot that sits on a terra cotta base. The tagine pot is designed to hold moisture and heat while cooking for long periods. Moroccans use seasonal vegetables and chicken, beef, mutton, or other meats in preparing tagine. They use a combination of spices which may differ depending on the vegetables and meat that is being prepared. Some typical spices might include garlic, cumin, ginger, curry, cinnamon, saffron, or turmeric. Olives and lemon zest are sometimes used to garnish the mixture or served on the large platter with couscous.[29]

Hahira Soup

Hahira soup is especially popular among Moroccans during Ramadan. The Moroccans have a bowl of Hahira soup to break the Ramadan fast each evening. Hahira soup is made with a tomato base, lamb's broth, and lentils or chick peas. It usually has celery, onion and garlic. Some Moroccans serve Hahira soup with *smen* which is very much like parmesan cheese. Hahira soup is seasoned with a combination of spices and herbs that may include pepper, cinnamon and ginger. Cilantro and parsley are sometimes used for extra flavor or as a garnish.[30]

The Milk Man

Larry and Margaret noticed a young man riding on a motorbike with three large cans of milk. He would stop in front of each house or apartment. There would be a jar placed beside the door and he would fill it with a dipper from one of his milk cans and move on to the next house.

Tea Customs

The tea and tea customs vary depending on whether one is having tea with someone from a British background or someone from a Moroccan background.

English Tea Customs

English tea customs reflect the influence of the British Empire.[31] English tea is usually served in an ironstone, porcelain, or china teapot. *Elevenses* or morning tea is sometimes offered to guests around mid-morning or may replace breakfast.[32] English tea is a brisk, black tea that is usually served with cream and sugar. Tea in the morning is usually served with sweet rolls, scones or tea biscuits.

Afternoon tea is typically served from 3:00 to 5:00 p.m.[33] Afternoon tea originated with the working class. The caffeine and sugar were intended to provide the necessary energy to complete a hard days' work. Afternoon tea may be served with small sandwiches, scones, or cakes such as Battenberg cake, fruit cake, or Victoria sponge cake. Battenberg cake is a light cake with alternate yellow and pink checkered patterns.[34] The layers have an apricot paste between them and the cake is covered in Marzipan, which is an almond paste. The chefs of the British Royal household first baked a Battenberg cake for Princess Victoria of Hesse and Prince Louis of Battenberg's marriage. A Victorian sponge cake is much like a pound cake with raspberry filling.[35]

High tea is usually served from 5:00 to 7:00.[36] High tea is usually served with a hot dish such as shepherd's pie or macaroni and cheese. This is sometimes followed by cakes and bread if dinner will not be served. High tea is sometimes an appetizer before dinner.

Moroccan Tea Customs

Moroccan Tea (Moroccan Whiskey)

Maghreb mint tea is a green tea with mint leaves and is sometimes called Moroccan whiskey even though it does not contain alcohol. Moroccan tea is generally served from a stainless steel or pewter teapot.[37] Moroccan tea is generally prepared by the men. It is served to the guest of honor first and it is considered rude to not drink the tea.[38] Larry and Margaret enjoyed making and drinking the Moroccan mint tea.[39]

Ramadan

Ramadan occurs during the ninth month of the Islamic calendar. It does not occur on the same dates every year, like Easter in America. The times are based on the lunar calendar. Muslims observe a fast from sunup to sundown during Ramadan. Ramadan is believed to be the time in which Mohammed received the Qur'an. Fasting during Ramadan is one of the Five Pillars of Islam. Moroccan law forbids anyone from eating, drinking water, or smoking publicly from sunup to sundown. Moroccans can be sent to prison for up to one year if they are seen eating publicly during fasting hours.

Businesses and schools open one hour late and close promptly at 4:00 p.m. to allow everyone to get home by sunset to break the fast. They have Hahira soup at sunset. At 9:30 p.m. a large meal is served. Everyone stays up until 1:00 a.m. Some Muslims arise at 4:30 a.m. to eat a large breakfast and to prepare for the day's fast.

One student who was coming to Larry and Margaret's apartment to learn English asked Larry to give the guidelines for the Christian's fast. Larry outlined Jesus's teachings, pointing out that Christians fasted privately. They bathe, dress and go about their work after they read the Bible and pray. In Morocco, the men do not shave in the morning. The women do not shampoo and arrange their hair or wear makeup during the thirty days of the fast. After hearing the Christian guidelines, the student remarked, "I do hope God will forgive us for doing it wrong"[40] (Larry & Margaret Rogers Newsletter, March 1994). The student went on to tell them that the Christian idea of praying for specific things during a fast was also different from the way that most Muslims observed Ramadan. He said that the fast was only a ritual to them.

One year Larry asked several of their Muslim acquaintances if he could come to their homes and take photographs during the Ramadan festival. They allowed him to photograph the festivities. Larry then took the photographs to these families and also gave them a Bible in either Arabic or French. They all received them gratefully and thanked him for the Bibles. Larry and Margaret along with friends and family prayed that God's Word would not return void.

Margaret wrote about several incidents in which the Moroccans became short-tempered and sometimes had serious altercations with each other, because they had not eaten all day and their blood sugar levels were low. Margaret told of one incident when they had gone to Tangier and were trying to catch a train. Several of the taxi drivers were quarreling in the street as Larry and Margaret walked past them. One of them intersected their path and asked where they were going. He could not understand that they wanted to catch a train so Margaret finally replied, "We are going to heaven!" Even though Heaven may not have been their immediate destination, the taxi driver decided that he could not take them there and left them alone.

The 26th day of Ramadan is when the Muslims believe that Allah gave the Qur'an to Muhammad the prophet.[41] The Muslims believe that Allah speaks to them in dreams and visions on this night of Ramadan. This night of the feast is called, 'The Night of Power.' [42] Many Christians have prayed during this night of the feast that the Muslims would see a vision of Jesus Christ and be drawn to Him. There have been numerous accounts of individuals who have had dreams and visions and have believed in Jesus Christ as a result of these dreams and visions. Larry and Margaret told about one young man who called a Christian friend of theirs who had experienced a vision of Jesus and desperately wanted to talk to a Christian about his vision. He was converted to Christianity after this experience.

Ramadan Ends

Ramadan ends when the moon is right. That might sound like a primitive calculation, but the Muslims wait until the new moon appears. The event is televised and a little boy plays his flute in the square at the mosque with a photograph of a new moon over him. When the new moon appears, the fast is over. Muslims begin dancing with joy![43]

There are feasts that occur after Ramadan officially ends such as the *Eid Fitr* and *Shawwal Al-Mukarram*. Eid Fitr is a thanksgiving feast to Allah and also a time of giving alms to the poor. There is a time of public prayer at the mosque. Shawwal Al-Mukarram is one of the grandest Muslim feasts. The feast follows six days of fasting. Fasting for six days after the Eid Fitr feast is the equivalent of fasting perpetually. According to the Muslims this fast will be rewarded ten times by Allah.

Ramadan Feasts

The Moroccans have a time of feasting in the evenings during Ramadan.[44] After they eat the Hahira soup, they may eat tagine, or another meat dish, breads and other foods. They bake special sweets and pastries for the Ramadan feasts. Ramadan is also a time when relatives and friends get together to visit and to celebrate much like families in America celebrate Christmas. There is usually loud music and dancing in the evenings to accompany the Ramadan festivities. Larry and Margaret found that it was impossible to sleep during Ramadan.

Aide Kbir Festival

Aide Kbir (the greater aid or the festival of sacrifice) is one of the most significant festivals to the Muslims. Aide Kbir is a celebration of the story of Abraham taking Ishmael to Mount Moriah to sacrifice him as he was attempting to show his complete obedience to God. When Abraham drew his knife to slay Ishmael, God spoke to him and called his attention to a ram that was caught in the thicket and instructed him not to harm Ishmael, but to sacrifice the ram instead. The Muslims call the son, Ishmael instead of Isaac.

Most of the Muslims purchase a sheep and keep him on their roofs for this occasion. The Muslims watch their televisions as the king slays his sheep to officially start this festival. All heads of families are expected to follow the king's example. After the sheep has been slain and dressed, the Muslims prepare a noon meal with the sheep's stomach.

On the first day of the festival, they lead the sheep out in the street to slay him inside the house where he is killed in their kitchens. They cut the sheep's head off and then take them to boys in the streets where they have fires going to burn the hair off the sheep and saw off the horns for 10 dirham each. The sheep is then gutted and the intestines are hung out to dry. Each family is supposed to eat the stomach and the liver the first day. The following days the family eats the remaining portions of the sheep. Even very poor families that may not have meat at other times during the year, purchase a sheep for Aide Kbir.

Larry and Margaret were invited to a Moroccan home to eat the sheep's head on one occasion. The family had served tea with cookies shortly before the meal. Larry had wisely held on to his cookies. When they began to serve the sheep head, Larry kept saying that he just wanted to keep eating the delicious cookies and managed not to have to eat the sheep's head. Margaret realized that the family considered the sheep's head to be a rare delicacy and thought that they were serving them something special. She managed to eat it and to compliment the cook on her wonderful recipe. The Muslims gather as the local Imam reads the account about Abraham and Ishmael and delivers a sermon and prayer for the occasion.

Larry and Margaret told several young people about the story of Jesus dying for our sins and how that he became our Pascal lamb. "Jesus is our Lamb," Margaret told one young man who did not understand why they did not celebrate this feast.[45]

Moroccan Weddings

Moroccan weddings, like most Middle Eastern weddings last for several days, sometimes up to a week. The bride-to-be is given a milk bath as a purification ritual the first day of the bridal week. The second day of the wedding week, the bride-to-be is given a bridal shower by the older women in the community. This is sometimes referred to as a "furnishing party." She is given household items much like a bridal shower in America.[47]

She is then given a Beberiska of her hands and feet. The Beberiska ceremony is an intricate process and the groom's name is usually painted in the designs.[47] A special henna artist, like a tattoo artist in America is hired for this ritual.[48] This ceremony is believed to ward off evil spirits from the couple's home and to increase fertility. This ceremony is sometimes referred to as a Henna party. There is music and dancing and guest's hands and feet are usually smeared with the paint that is used on the bride-to-be.[49]

The third day of the wedding week, the groom presents the bride with gifts. These gifts may range from lowly kitchen staples such as flour and sugar to elaborate clothes and jewelry depending on his economic status. The day of the wedding, the attendants dress the bride-to-be in her wedding kaftan and jewelry, fix her hair and makeup and place the veil on her head.[50] Unlike American weddings; the bride has several kaftans and will change her kaftan several times throughout the day of the wedding.[51]

Moroccans say that it is good luck for the bride to walk around the house three times where she and the groom will live before the ceremony. The bride is carried to the wedding ceremony by young men on a platform called an amaria.[52] This ritual is called the *berza* or the presentation of the bride.

The groom appears wearing either a *jabadoor* (tunic and pants) or a suit.[53] An Islamic Imam performs the wedding ceremony. Only the bride and groom are present for the ceremony. After the ceremony, the groom is carried to the bridal chamber by his attendants on their shoulders and the bride is carried to the bridal chamber on the amaria.

There is a huge wedding feast that is usually catered.[54] Some of the traditional wedding foods include pigeon pie, lamb with roasted almonds and hard boiled eggs or chicken with olives and lemon. [55]The guests are served milk and dates when they arrive. Milk is symbolic of purity and dates are symbolic of happiness. Pastries, cookies and biscotti are served for desert. There is loud music and dancing. Moroccan wedding lamps adorn the tables.[56]

Margaret wrote about several Moroccan weddings that they attended. One wedding was to begin at 9:00 p.m. They drove to the house where the wedding was to take place and noticed that the bride-to-be and her sisters were at the beauty shop next to their house. Most of the brides rent a house for the wedding ceremony. Lights are typically strung all over the porch outside like Americans might string lights at Christmas.

Larry and Margaret had to wait for the beautician to fix the girls' hair and apply their make-up. They went on to the house to wait with the girls' mother. She only spoke Arabic. The groom and his father came in and greeted Larry and Margaret. They spoke English. The groom left about 10:00 p.m. to go to meet the wedding party.

The house was like many Moroccan homes. It had beautiful tile work, wood decorative ceilings, but no heat. The night of the wedding was one of the coldest that Larry and Margaret remembered. The women were escorted to one room for eating and dancing. The men were escorted to another room. Sometimes if the houses are smaller, a curtain or some sort of divider is placed in the room and the women would meet on one side and the men on the other.

The bride's procession did not start until after midnight and the groom rode in on his horse. The band got started after about another hour. When it was time for the procession to enter the house where the ceremony was to be held, the music began to crescendo. After they entered the house the women began a fashion show as they paraded across the room in one of their colorful jalabas or kaftans. They would go behind a curtain and change to another jalaba or kaftan after they danced across the room and displayed the first costume. They would usually change about six or seven times during the wedding. These outfits are usually rented unless the family is wealthy. Margaret commented that she was about to get up and teach them the jitterbug in order to keep warm.

Larry and Margaret did not have a wedding jalaba and they felt somewhat out of place. Margaret remarked that she felt like the person that Jesus talked about who did not have a wedding garment. She also thought of the ten virgins that Jesus talked about in Matthew waiting for the bridegroom to come in to the late hours of the night. Most Moroccan weddings last until 5:00 a.m.

The little round tables were covered with white table clothes embroidered in pink with matching napkins. They used silverware for the wedding. The first course was a round platter as big as a number 2 washing tub with what looked like a half of a lamb. Each plate had a round piece of bread that they were to scoop the contents out of the round platter on to their plates.[57] Margaret remarked that it was the most delicious meal she had ever eaten.[58] A teacher friend sat next to her and the hostess kept putting large portions on her plate and telling her that they expected her to eat. One of them told her that they had heard all about their nice American neighbor.

The next item on the menu was a large platter of baked chicken. Then the waiters brought dessert, an ice cream cake. They all exclaimed, "Ice cream! Ice cream!" They were each given a spoon and quickly consumed the ice cream cake from the same platter. The waiters then delivered a huge bowl of beautiful fresh fruit. After they had eaten the fruit, the waiters began to remove the tables and set up the instruments for the orchestra. The orchestra began to play and the groom and all of his groomsmen along with Larry came in with lit candles and bearing the huge brass coiffeurs that contained gifts for the bride. The gifts were placed with great pomp and circumstances in the large salon area where the ladies were seated. The wedding cake was delivered. The music continued as the wedding party waited for the bride to arrive at midnight.

The groom was carried in on his throne like chair and at midnight the special horns sounded outside, the candle torches were lit and the young men in white entered bearing the bride in the special seat on their shoulders. They marched and danced around with the bride to the tempo of the music. The bride was wearing a beautiful white kaftan and decked with jewels as she smiled and waved to everyone.The orchestra erupted in rapturous music and the girls arose and started dancing. Cameras began flashing to catch the excitement. Waiters kept busy passing out water and juices to drink. Then they began to serve mint tea and fancy cookies.

The King's Birthday

The Moroccans celebrate the king's birthday, August 21st with great fanfare. All schools and businesses close for the king's birthday. The following YouTube link shows a video clip of the king's birthday celebration in 1993, the first year that Larry and Margaret saw it.[59]

The present king, Mohammed VI is given credit for increasing job opportunities and for modernizing transportation and other parts of the Moroccan infrastructure. Some argue that much of the propaganda that is circulated about his reforms is exaggerated. The birthday celebration is marked with festivals, parades, feasting and dancing.

English Bookstore

Larry and Margaret were delighted to find an English bookstore soon after they arrived in Fes. The gentleman who owned the store told them how to get to an English-speaking church. They attended this church and were introduced to other Christians from several denominations who were there as undercover missionaries. They were most grateful for the opportunity to find an English-speaking church. Since Christians must be undercover in Muslim countries, churches do not have signs, websites, or phone numbers listed in the yellow pages. These are the normal means by which a tourist would find a church. Christians are naturally skeptical of strangers who ask about their religion or place of worship because they recognize the dangers of divulging information about their faith.

Moroccan Death Customs

The most tragic story that Larry and Margaret were involved with involved the death of a little five-year-old boy whom they had grown to love. This child would spot Larry and Margaret coming down the

108

street and would yell to them calling them uncle and aunt. He was the nephew of one of the interpreters that helped them in the beginning.

The child was sent home from school one day with a high fever. His mother asked her brother-in-law who was a doctor to stop by to check on him. The doctor came and thought that he may have food poisoning. His temperature continued to rise and the family noticed that he was covered with black spots. The family took him to the hospital. His uncle and a pediatrician at the hospital examined him. The child died the next morning. At first, they thought that the child had meningitis. His sister also had a high fever and she was placed in the hospital for observation for six days and given medications.

The doctors later determined that the child had died from pupura fulminous caused by the virus meningocoque. This infection causes severe hemorrhaging, low blood pressure, fever and a severe decrease in the platelet count. They later learned that the child had contracted the virus from a pet turtle.

Larry and Margaret prayed with the family and tried to comfort them. Exactly one year later, the parents had another son. Larry and Margaret attended a huge feast that they had in the son's honor. The men who carry the corpse carry it high above their heads. The corpse is wrapped in a white sheet and tied at the head and foot. An afghan is wrapped around the sheet. They cut holes in the sheet for the eyes, nose and mouth. The men that are family and friends follow the men carrying the corpse to the burial. The women remain at home mourning.

Moroccans usually bury the dead within twenty-four hours. The body is buried facing Mecca. The family and friends meet for a meal a couple of days later. The mourning period is forty days. Muslims wear white during mourning instead of black as has been the tradition in America.[60]

One of the neighbors told Larry that his father-in-law had cancer. Larry offered to go pray with the man but the son-in-law did not invite him to come. A few days later, the son-in-law told Larry that his father-in-law had died during the night. He asked Larry to come to speak to the family. Larry and Margaret went to the family's home where they were playing the Islamic death chant on the stereo. The family invited them to join them for coffee.

The daughter brought in the incense and passed it around the room. She then went around and sprinkled everyone in the room with sweet smelling orange blossom water. The daughter then went to the room where the corpse was and began to wail loudly. Margaret went in to join her and wept with her. The body was to be moved to the mosque by noon and then buried by 2:00 p.m.

Larry and Margaret watched later that day as the funeral procession started for the mosque. Only the men followed the procession to the grave site while the women returned to their homes. Margaret visited the widow and daughters the following week and prayed with them.

Easter Sunday

Margaret wrote about the first Easter, 1993 when they were in Morocco. She woke up and began to sing, "Christ the Lord is Risen Today—Hallelujah!" She looked outside and could see the dejected looking Moroccans wandering the dirty streets just as they did any other day. She read the account in the Bible about the women preparing the spices to go to the tomb. As she was reading this account, she looked out and saw a woman preparing spices with a mortar and pestle and screen just like they would have done at the time of Christ. She saw donkeys with their carts of merchandise coming to the market and talked about how realistic the setting was for Easter morning in this eastern setting. They went to the English-speaking church and enjoyed worshipping with other Christians and singing the traditional Easter hymns and having fellowship with their Christian friends after church. They were constantly made aware of the fact that there was a void among the Moroccan people, because they had not accepted the resurrected Christ. They only proclaimed that he was a good prophet.

Prayer and Outreach Focus

There have been numerous testimonies of Muslims who have had visions and have seen dreams that have caused them to believe in the resurrected Christ. Pray for a spiritual hunger among the Muslim people. Pray against the powers of evil in this region of North Africa. Pray for a movement of the Holy Spirit among the North Africans to convict them of sin and to draw them to Christ. Pray that missionaries in this region will have opportunities to share the gospel.

Larry and Margaret with Renault truck.

Larry and Margaret's apartment building.

Kathy and Margaret discussing English as a second language.

Kathy-The British midwife that Margaret and Larry knew in her lemon orchard.

Chapter Fourteen

The Bullfight

🌹

If I fought wild beast in Ephesus for merely human reasons, what have I gained? (I Corinthians 15:32).

Margaret wrote about the bullfight that they attended in Malaga during the week of the fiesta. The women of all ages wore the traditional ruffled long dresses and danced in the streets. Their escorts rode on horses and sometimes the ladies with the ruffled dresses rode behind the escort on a horse. Others rode on motorcycles. There is a bullfight every night of the festival in the bullring.[1]

Bullfighting is the national sport in Spain. The object of the sport is for the matador to kill the wild bull with a sword. Animal activists have protested bullfighting in recent years, but have not been successful in doing away with this popular sport. The best known bullfight is the one that is held in Seville each year.

Many ancient civilizations practiced bullfighting or some variation of the sport. The Minoans, the Greeks, the Romans and other cultures had bullfights before the Spanish. We are not certain if Paul's reference to fighting wild beasts in Ephesus is to be taken figuratively or literally. There is not a specific scriptural reference to him being thrown to the lions. However, it was common for early Christians to be thrown to the lions and for spectators to watch as they battled the lions in the arena. Margaret said that she thought about the early Christians and the Roman gladiators when they went to the bullfight.[2]

The Plaza de Toros de la Maestranza in Seville was constructed in the late 1700's and has served as the primary bullfighting arena since then. [3] The Plaza de Toros de la Maestranza in Seville can seat about 12,500 spectators. Even though this arena is not the largest, many tourists choose to go to the Plaza de Toros de la Maestranza in Seville because of its history and glamour. [4] La Plaza de Toros de Las Ventas in Madrid is the largest bullfighting arena and can seat 25,000 spectators. La Plaza de Toros de Las Ventas in Madrid is a more modern structure. [5]

The bullfighting season only lasts a few weeks and is accompanied by a festival. Local merchants sell their wares and food vendors line the streets selling their specialties. Musicians entertain the crowds and sell instruments and CDs. The girls wear long dresses with ruffles and flowers in their hair. They danced in the streets. Escorts brought some of the girls in on horses. Some even came in on motorcycles, holding up their long dresses to keep the ruffles out of the wheels.

As Larry and Margaret were waiting for the bullfight to begin, some young children seated next to them were entertaining them with jokes. "How do you keep the bull from charging?" one asked. He read the answer to his joke since no one responded, "You take away his credit card." Margaret commented that this child was not in a jovial mood after the bullfight. The blood and gore were too much for most adults to handle. Children really should not have witnessed such violence.

The procession began with the band playing as three horse drawn coaches entered with the girls in their ruffled dresses. After the girls exited all of the matadors entered riding the padded horse to spear the bulls. The band played more lively music; the gate opened and in galloped the first frisky bull where several matadors waved the Spanish flags. As the bull charged, they darted behind screens. Then the master matador came out with a red flag and a sword. The spearman entered on the blindfolded padded horse. The matador coaxed the bull over to the horse where the man speared him right in the back. Another matador came out to help with the teasing. One by one they struck two spears each in the bulls back near to where the first spear was inserted. The teasing continued until the bull was worn down. Then the master matador sunk the final sword in the bull's head. The bull, bleeding profusely, fell over dead. Blindfolded horses with chain pulleys were led in to drag off the carcasses. The janitors then came to clean up the mess. The process was repeated until all six bulls had entered and been killed by the matadors. The process took about fifteen minutes for each bull for the bullfight that Larry and Margaret witnessed.

One lady explained to them that the bulls that were in the ring were raised on a large farm where they were free to roam in large pastures for six years until they were brought in for a bullfight. She went on to say that if she were a bull, she would rather be free to roam large pastures for six years and die gallantly in the ring rather than to be cooped up and taken to slaughter to die for food and leather. Many Spaniards do not share this lady's thinking.

Margaret remembered that she and her sisters were afraid of the bulls on the neighbor's farm in Asbury, North Carolina when they were small children. Their mother had warned them not to go near the bulls. As she witnessed her first bullfight, she understood why her mother had insisted that the children avoid these ferocious creatures.

Apparently, bullfighting is not nearly as dangerous as it was in more ancient times, which probably accounts for the fact that the sport seems to be losing some popularity. There are always young men waiting to carry out someone that is injured to a rescue squad. Doctors are usually available if immediate assistance is needed. In ancient times, the matadors would fight until they were killed or the bull was killed.

Missionaries in North Africa may not be thrown to the lions as were the Christians in Rome, but they do face intense persecution, deportment, prison and other tortures if they are reported for trying to convert Muslims to Christianity.

Prayer and Outreach Focus
Pray for divine protection for our missionaries in North Africa.

Chapter Fifteen

Castor Beans, English as Second Language & Friendship Evangelism

I no longer call you servants, because a servant does not know his master's business. Instead, I call you friends, for everything that I learned from my Father I have made known to you (John 15:15).

Larry and Margaret needed to choose a cover for their missionary venture before leaving for Morocco since Morocco is an Islamic country and missionaries are not allowed to enter the country. Larry decided to go as an agricultural consultant for a castor bean project. Margaret went as a teacher. She would teach English as a second language.

Larry and Margaret had some of their own challenges learning the Arabic and French languages that were spoken in Morocco. Larry started a project to help to clean up the streets. He would go out early in the mornings on the days that the trash men were to come and gather the garbage that had been left in the streets. On hot mornings, Larry would meet the trash men with cold ice water to help quench their thirst. Some of the neighbors began to follow Larry's example and would meet him in the streets each morning to pick up trash. One man said to Larry, "Welcome to you with all my heart" one morning. Larry responded with what he thought was a similar greeting and everyone began to laugh heartily. The greeting that he had returned was, "Welcome to you with all my dog!" Heart and dog apparently have similar pronunciations in Arabic.

Margaret once learned that she had been using the incorrect word for babies. She was calling babies "turkeys". She wondered why the mothers were frowning at her when she commented about their babies. These struggles helped them to empathize with the Moroccan students who would struggle so diligently to learn English. Margaret had no difficulty finding students who were interested in learning English. Everywhere they went people would stop them as soon as they heard them speaking English and want them to allow them to practice their English. They could not leave their apartment or go to the Medina without people stopping them to speak English.

Morocco is a highly cosmopolitan country. They met individuals who were Spanish, French, Dutch, German and Arabic. They met people from Nigeria and other African states. They met Catholics and Protestants, Jews and Muslims. Morocco is a great melting pot and all of these people wanted to learn to speak English. The unemployment rate especially among younger people is high in Morocco and many younger people saw the opportunity to learn English as their ticket to America where they would have better job opportunities.

Teaching English as a Second Language and Our Holy Book

One evening near 6:00, which was the tea time in Morocco, their doorbell rang. Margaret answered it and found the neighbor's oldest son at the door. He came in and said that his mother had asked him to see if Margaret had some oil that she could share. Margaret immediately got out the olive oil and sent her a generous portion. The young man quickly left so that his mother could make their bread for tea. Then Margaret wondered if the mother had flour and other staple goods. The next day Margaret decided to go over to visit the lady and discovered that they were in dire need of food. Larry and Margaret went out and gathered the main food staples and took them to her. She was most grateful and asked if she could come and practice her English with Margaret. Margaret assured her that she was welcome to come to their apartment to practice her English. When she came, she asked if Margaret had a book in English that she could share with her to read. Margaret promptly asked her if she would like to read their Holy Book in English. She responded that she would be happy to have it to read.

She returned the next day and was so happy to tell that she had read most of the Gospels and that it gave her peace. However, she said that there were some things that she did not understand. Then she asked if Margaret could meet with her at least twice a week to explain to her the things that she did not understand. As these sessions continued her understanding opened and she said that she really believed in the Word. She would always ask for prayer at the end of each session. Then one day she brought a friend with her who could not speak English. Margaret invited her Dutch friend to join these sessions as the interpreter of the friend's French. This friend was very quick to accept the Word and took the Holy Book in French home with her and placed it on her chest each night as she slept. She said that it gave her great peace and she was able to sleep peacefully.

Margaret then began to set aside Fridays as the time that she and her Dutch friend met each week to open up these truths to them. As the meetings continued the women brought more until they had a nice size class. Soon the first two women asked if they could have water baptism and asked that Margaret and her Dutch friend baptize them. Margaret explained to them that she and her friend would not do the baptism, but would introduce them to some of their own people that believed the Word to do the baptism. They invited a lovely woman from their own country to join them for the Friday class. She came for three weeks until she and the women were convinced that they trusted each other. The baptism was scheduled to occur in one of the apartments where the group met each Sunday. Margaret and her friend accepted the invitation to join them in order to see the baptism. Ordinarily foreigners do not join them for their meeting because it would call attention to the meeting of the group that might lead to the police coming to arrest them. The foreigners could also be deported. There were more baptisms that followed as these believers shared their faith with others.

The English Class

When Larry and Margaret first went to North Africa they discovered that there were many of the young people taking English in their schools and universities. When these people discovered that Larry and Margaret spoke English, they approached them and asked if Margaret would teach an English class in their apartment. Margaret began looking through materials she had brought from the states for an appropriate curriculum. She soon chose the Frank Laubauch series over one that used the Bible as the text. She thought this series would be safer. When she arose the next morning having her devotions and reading from the Word the Lord brought the verse from Romans 1:15 to her mind, "...for I am not ashamed of the gospel of Christ. . . ." She immediately knew that she must change to the curriculum that used the Bible as the text. She knew that if someone reported her to government officials that she could face imprisonment, severe beating and torture. She could even face death or at the least deportment. She had heard of other missionaries who had been deported and imprisoned for distributing Bibles or witnessing about Christianity. She had heard of others that had been tortured and murdered. She felt strongly that she should teach and distribute the Word despite the potential consequences.

She laid out the Holy Book on the table for the young man who assisted in preparing materials for class to take to the copier to make copies for the night class. When Larry passed through the room he exclaimed, "Margaret, you are not going to use this curriculum, are you?" Margaret explained what the Lord had spoken to her that morning during her devotional time. Larry relaxed and said, "Okay, the Lord will take care of it."

There were ten students that showed up for the class. For an entire year the classes met regularly. Often only half the class would arrive on time and the others would just drop in several minutes or even an hour later. Margaret started the classes on time and made room for the late ones to pick up the lesson sheets and to join them when they arrived. They learned rapidly and one of the young women progressed to become the English teacher at an elementary school nearby. Another great achiever was a young man who improved his English and was able to get a job in the office at a construction business on the coast. Larry and Margaret always made themselves available for anyone seeking guidance in prayer or to read and discuss the Word.

The young woman who had become an English teacher later went to Spain and got a job. One foggy morning as she was attempting to cross a busy street, she was hit by a car and killed. Her body was brought back to Morocco city for burial. As Margaret heard of this tragedy she and some of the women from the class were gathered at her apartment. The men were taking the coffin out for burial. Only the men go to the burial. The women stay at home to mourn while tea and sweets are served at intervals. As Margaret and the small group of women walked along the street to their apartments she assured them that the girl was in heaven with the Lord and that they would see her again.

Larry heard that some of the officials were making remarks about using the Holy Book as a text for the class. Larry felt that the class should not continue to use the Holy Book. Larry and Margaret lived just across the street from one of the police stations and they were too visible to continue to openly use the Holy Book if the authorities had become suspicious. The class did not meet formally after they decided that they were perhaps under scrutiny but individuals continued to come to seek help with their English as well as with questions about the Holy Book. Larry and Margaret would give the students Bibles as part of their training. Every time they crossed the border with boxes or suitcases loaded with Bibles they would pray and others would pray for their safety. The Lord protected them each time and the Bibles and other religious literature that they smuggled in the country were never confiscated.

Larry kept a stash of Bibles hidden in their apartment. There were numerous people in addition to the English language students who would come to their apartment for counseling and for other needs. Larry would always give them a Bible and pray with them. Larry and Margaret soon found that the Muslims welcomed prayer but they did not understand why Christians prayed, 'in Jesus's name.' They would often resist their prayers when they learned that they prayed to Jesus. Some of them would come back when their situations became desperate and ask them to pray. They saw that Larry and Margaret's prayers were being answered.

One Jewish lady asked Margaret to tutor her twelve year old son. Margaret agreed to tutor the boy and became friends with the mother. The mother had surgery for a brain tumor and realized that she needed to walk in order to improve her coordination and strength. She wanted to walk with Margaret and Margaret readily agreed even though the lady's pace was very slow at first. Margaret used the time that she was with her to talk to her about the Lord. She noticed when she would go to their apartment that the mother would be watching the television on the European Christian Broadcasting Network channel.

Larry and Margaret learned of a girl who was very poor and needed money. They learned that she had cleaned houses so they asked her to help them one day a week to provide her with some much needed funds. She desperately wanted to learn English. She told Margaret that when someone would call and she and Larry were not at the apartment that they would hang up if she answered the phone in Arabic. She wanted to learn English so that she could answer the phone for them in English. Margaret immediately began to tutor her. After just a few lessons, Margaret would meet her at the door with a simple sentence like, "Hello, I'm Margaret. Who are you?" She would respond with her name and then ask Margaret a question in English.

Friendship with a British Midwife

Larry and Margaret were fascinated with a white haired British midwife that was always in their gathering for worship. They wanted to visit their friend in her home in the old part of the city. They started a special prayer group in their apartment in another part of the city and met once a week to encourage each other. This lady from Britain heard of the prayer group and wanted to join them.

Larry and Margaret got to know her and learned that she came as a young woman trained as a surgical nurse and midwife. Others had come with a similar background and had set up a place in a large house in the old part of the city where they could reach and serve the people in that area. As the years passed all of them had moved on and she was left alone in the big house. She had an amazing wealth of stories to share of their experiences.

They had delivered many babies for the families all around them and everyone felt free to come to the big house to discuss their problems. They set up a place of worship in the basement of the big house and met there for worship each Sunday. Many were touched and believed the Word. A baptistery was set up in the basement to baptize those who requested it. One day a fellow believer, who worked for the government, was in a meeting in the capitol area. He overheard one ask the king what he was going to do about the two women in the old city in our area who were having worship services in their midwife's clinic. The king responded that it should be closed.

After this meeting the believer rushed out and caught the train to the old part of the city. He went to the pastor of the expatriate group and related the story. The pastor immediately made the trip into the old city to the big house to warn the midwives. They received him and thanked him for the warning. However they were wondering what should be done. They wanted to trust the Lord to protect this gathering. It was Saturday night and just before retiring as their custom was to read from the little book called *Bread* one of them picked it up and turned to the devotional for the day. The verse was from Isaiah 26:20: "Come my people. Enter your chambers and shut your door behind you, hide yourself as it were for a little moment until the indignation is past." This was a stunning verse and they realized that it was God's warning for them and the worship group. They began to make plans to arise the next morning; one would go one way and the other another way and warn the believers not to come to the big house that day. This took the greater part of the morning and nearing noon they slowly began walking back to the big house. As they came into view of the entrance leading to the house they observed soldiers standing at both ends guarding the place. They went back and stopped in to visit markets as though they were shopping for things.

Keeping a close watch out of the corner of their eyes they soon saw that it was near 12:00 noon and the soldiers began to depart in order to get their lunch. This gave them an opportunity to enter the big house and share their stories. Thankfully the warning had been successful. Everyone was safe.

The group did not meet at the big house after this episode. However the greater part of the group went outside the city and found a cave in which they could worship in secret. Remnants of the group scattered to other parts of the city and found places where they could worship in secret. Larry and Margaret were fortunate to meet some members of these groups. Many had suffered prison terms. Larry and Margaret's friend told about being sent to prison several times and being beaten and forced to drink her own urine. The police are still watching others where ever they go. One great note is that they all stand firm. What a legacy!

Larry's Personal Contacts

The apostle Paul had an effective evangelism strategy that he used in Athens that Larry decided to utilize in Morocco. Paul was in the marketplace daily. He built up a rapport with the merchants. The marketplace was a gathering place where people came to debate the issues of the day and to discuss philosophy and religion. Paul knew that these scholars and merchants would not come to the synagogue so he went to them. He joined in their discussions. He had compassion on their needs. He prayed for them. Larry began walking around the old Medina shortly after they moved to their apartment. This area is a heavy populated area in a section of the old city. He discovered that there were several small businesses where he heard English being spoken as he passed by on his walk. He began to stop in to examine their wares and would buy a little something each day. He found the merchants to be quite interested in talking to him as a foreigner that spoke English. This led to friendships and as he began to build a rapport with the merchants, they would ask questions about personal problems and difficulties they faced each day. On some occasions he was invited back into a private office where they could talk to him privately about their special needs. At such times Larry shared with them about the love of God and that He was interested in helping them solve these daily needs.

They believed that God was a supreme being in His heaven that did not have time for personal problems. Larry patiently took his time to explain to them about the love of God and offered to share with them from his Holy Book the special Words of Life. One young man shared that he could not make enough money to get married to the girl he had be seeing for ten years. Larry assured him that he would be praying for him that God would work it out for his salary to increase so that he could get married. He was very puzzled and told Larry that God did not have time to take care of matters like that. Larry calmly replied, "You will see."

Shortly after Larry's prayer with this young man, Larry and Margaret made a trip to the states for a few months. As they returned Larry made a quick trip into the city market to get supplies. As he was gathering things to purchase he heard a voice in the distance, "Hello, Mr. Larry." Looking in the direction of that voice he spotted his young friend who was rushing up to greet him. He had a young woman with him and exclaimed, "I want you to meet my wife! It is all your fault," he said laughingly. There were many other stories that came from this regular walk in this part of the city. Larry was so grateful to find an area where he could dialogue in his own language. This became one of his main ministry opportunities while he was in Morocco.

Larry's Castor Bean Project

Larry's castor bean project was a bit of a challenge. He had prayed about this project and felt that this was the venue that he should choose. It seemed difficult for him to make contacts at first with individuals about this project. He continued to pray and God began to open doors with complete strangers in a foreign country.[1]

Larry Consults with King's Consultant

Margaret wrote about Larry's first opportunity to share about his castor bean project with the king's consultant. One day they had an appointment in the capitol city and were returning from Spain traveling by ferry across the Mediterranean Sea. The first train that they could catch got them into the station just as it was getting dark. A well-dressed man on the train had joined them in the compartment supposedly to practice his English. He was quite inquisitive as to where they were going when they got off the train.

They tried to shake him off as they got off the train, but to no avail. He grabbed their suitcases and hailed a taxi posing as a helper. He told the driver that he was helping them to a hotel. He then reverted to speaking their language which Larry and Margaret did not understand at the time. They became suspicious about the long distance the driver was taking them. Finally he asked the driver to stop the taxi, jumped out to get the suitcases and told them to wait there as he had contacted a hotel that was sending a van to transport them to the city. As Larry opened up his wallet to pay the fare and handed it to the driver the man grabbed a big share of money from Larry's wallet and was quickly on his way. It was dark and they stood alone on a dimly lit street supposedly waiting for a van. After a few minutes they realized that this guy was a thief and began to send up some S.O.S. prayers to God.

After some time they saw two men coming down the road from their night prayers and one walked over speaking in fluent English. He asked if they were waiting for someone and Larry related their story to him. He was appalled and quickly hailed a passing taxi and took them to a hotel. He helped them into the hotel and explained to the clerk what had happened. The clerk was very sympathetic and sent his worker to take their suitcases up to their room as well as sending them soft drinks. The kind helper just quietly disappeared who had paid the taxi fee. Margaret believes that this man was truly an angel that the Lord had sent to their defense.

The next morning Larry left early for his appointment leaving Margaret in the hotel room to pray for his success. Larry met with the king's consultant who told him that the king had been looking for an agriculture product to take the place of marijuana that was being grown in the north of the country. He instructed Larry to secure seeds for them to plant on the experimental farms.

King Hassan II gave Larry an official stamped document from the agronomy department chair. Larry could carry this document with him anywhere he went on his frequent trips to the University of Rabat, the capitol city. He would often take Bibles with him when he would go to the university to distribute to young people who were interested in his faith.

On their return to Morocco they were joined by two young men in their compartment on the train. They were university students returning home for the weekend and enjoyed speaking to them in English. One of them was the son of a business man and he was quite interested in hearing Larry tell about the castor bean project. He said that his father would be interested. In a few days Larry had a phone call from the business man who arranged an interview with him in Meknes.

He sent his chauffer to pick up Larry. He was escorted to a plush office. Larry presented his business plan for the castor bean project as the man eagerly listened. Larry left some information with him. The man insisted on taking Larry to dinner at a five-star hotel near his office. After dinner another chauffeur took them to a farm outside of Meknes. He showed Larry a plot of land where he could plant his castor beans and introduced him to the farmers who would do the work for him. He was told to order his seed and to have the farmers to plant them in March.

Larry's agricultural project, growing castor beans was also accepted by the University of Rabat in January, 1994. He was told to get the seed and to have an experimental crop planted. He ordered the seeds from Texas and they were planted on three experimental farms in March. As a consultant for this project, he obtained marketing and pricing information. Larry met a young man who had a Ph.D. in agricultural engineering who accompanied him to the university and to the farm. This young man spoke fluent Arabic and French and gave instructions to the farmers and students at the university about planting and developing the castor bean crop.

The first year, they planted one hundred rows of castor beans on the Meknes farm. A professor at Virginia Polytechnic Institute and State University assisted Larry with directing the research and collating the data for this project. Larry soon realized that he desperately needed a vehicle to go back and forth to supervise the three experimental castor bean projects. Some individuals in the states heard about this need and quickly rallied to the cause. Within a few months, churches and individuals had raised the funds for Larry and Margaret to purchase a Renault truck.

They were most grateful for this gift not only to use with the agricultural project, but for their many other transportation needs. Other missionaries and students called on them frequently to take them to medical appointments, to the embassy and to the train, or ferry.

Larry went to the castor fields at the end of the summer. He met with his young Ph.D. friend who helped to direct the farmers to gather the seeds, count them and to store them in the barns. He met with the business man in Meknes to give him a report on the yield.

The next summer was an extremely hot summer without rain until the country suffered from a terrific drought. The king cancelled all experimental agricultural projects that year in order to save water for the food crops.

Residency

Larry and Margaret were devastated when the castor bean project was canceled. They knew that they would be forced to leave if they could not have a cover for their work. They prayed to the Lord to make a way for them to get their residency. They had an appointment at the consulate about their residency. They sat for hours wondering just what would happen. They had brought two friends with them to talk with the officers in charge who spoke fluent French and Arabic. They could hear the officer questions the friends in a mocking sort of way and got the indication that this man was not going to do anything to help them.

The officer in charge of this department was severely stern and liked to demonstrate his authority. When their turn came and they went into his office and gave him the folder containing all of their important documents, he surveyed them and began barking comments about the fact that they had to have a reason for being in the country and if they did not have a legitimate reason to be there, they would have to leave. They knew that he had told some to leave the country within 48 hours. At this point, Margaret broke into tears while Larry kept his masculine composure. The man paused a few seconds and then began leafing through the folder. On the very top of the folder was Margaret's retirement document from the school system. He poured over that for a few minutes and then remarked, "Retiree, retiree—you could be here as retirees." What a miracle! He calmed down and instructed them to make the trip into the American Embassy on the coast to get a document declaring that they were retired. They left triumphantly knowing that the Lord had worked it out for them to be there and be free from daily business schedules enabling them to visit and make contacts with people there. God knew how to work out the whole situation.

The Mid-Atlas Mountains

Larry and Margaret made several visits to the Mid Atlas Mountains to visit the Berbers. It was usually cold and often snowing at this higher plateau. The Berbers are a nomadic people. They move their herds to the lower plateau in the winter and to the higher plateau for grazing in the summer.[2]

The black goat's hair tents looked like something that may have existed in Old Testament times. The people were hospitable, but somewhat suspicious of foreigners. The first time Larry and Margaret and another couple went up to visit the Berbers, Margaret and the lady with her decided that they should tie scarves around their heads like the Berber women were wearing, so that they would have their heads covered like they did. They were trying to fit in as much as possible so that the Berbers would accept them. When they were returning to their car, a man came rushing after them angrily shouting something that indicated that he thought that Larry and the man with him were kidnapping some of their women. When he caught up with them, the ladies removed their head coverings and convinced him that they were not Berbers. They did not realize that they looked so authentic.

They soon built a rapport with the Berbers. The Berbers came out of their tents to meet them and gave them a Berber handshake. The Berbers only touch the tip of your fingers and then kiss their fingers. Many of the tents were flea infested as the camels, goats, sheep and other animals were right around the tents. The first day they visited one of the tents they promised to return the next day with medication for insect bites. The Berbers were most grateful when they returned with the medication that they found at a pharmacy in a nearby town.

When Larry and Margaret returned the following day, they were invited in the tent to sit on the wool rugs on the ground. A skinny dog faintly walked in the tent and began to lick the crumbs off of the low table where Larry and Margaret were going to eat lunch. The Berber woman milked two of the goats, scrambled eggs for them and served them with some barley bread that she had made. She then boiled water to make tea for them. By this time, the grandmother had returned with some of the children and their herd of goats. The goats decided to seek shelter from the afternoon sun and wondered inside the tent.

Larry and Margaret realized that there were many needs among these people for food, clothing, supplies and medical attention. They did what they could to help to meet their physical needs. Larry found that they enjoyed oranges and he would take them oranges when he would visit along with some clothes or whatever he knew that they needed.

The Berbers had not heard about Christianity and most were eager to learn. Larry and Margaret gathered as many battery-operated tape recorders as they could find when they came to the states and took them to the Berbers along with tapes in their language. Most of them are illiterate.

Christmas in Morocco

Larry and Margaret had never lived anywhere before where the people did not celebrate Christmas. There were no decorations, no parties and no special Christmas treats. Margaret wrote that Luke's account of the angel's message to the shepherds was very real in Morocco. Shepherds with their flocks passed by their apartment each morning to find pasture in the nearby fields. They watched shepherds faithfully guarding their sheep as they went out each day. These people have a simple life. Their primary meat is mutton and they sheer the sheep for wool blankets.

Larry and Margaret found particular hope in Isaiah's prophecy the first year that they were in Morocco. Larry's vision that he had before going to Morocco talked about a people who were bent on destruction. They read Isaiah 9:2 with new hope in the Christmas of 1993 ". . . on those living in the land of the shadow of death a light has dawned." They found that many of the Moroccans wanted to escape their dark worlds. They wanted to hear the message that the light had dawned.

Larry and Margaret would place an olive wood nativity scene on their buffet each Christmas. When the Moroccans would come to visit them they would always notice the nativity scene and would ask questions about the figures in the scene. This gave Larry and Margaret an opportunity to tell them about the birth of Jesus.

Margaret decorated a small artificial Christmas tree with lights and olive wood ornaments. The lighted Christmas tree quickly became quite a conversation piece. Larry and Margaret would explain the significance of the tree to the Moroccans who would inquire about it. Larry had given one young man a suit some time earlier and he told them that he wanted to go home and put on his suit and have Larry to take his picture with the tree. He wanted to send the photograph to his girlfriend. Several of the other young men who were with him wanted to have their photographs taken with the Christmas tree, too.

The first year that Larry and Margaret were in Morocco, another missionary took them to visit the Children's Haven Orphanage in the mountains. This missionary had started a tradition of going to the orphanage each Christmas to take the children candy and special treats. The children rewarded them with a beautiful Christmas program. Sixteen Moroccan youth presented the Christmas story both in song and narration in perfect English. Larry and Margaret continued this tradition when the other missionary could not be there and other missionaries continued to go after Larry and Margaret were not able to travel.

The missionaries who work at the orphanage are the only missionaries in Morocco who are not under cover. They are permitted to be there as missionaries because of the work that they do with the children who would otherwise be homeless. There is no foster system or any other provision for orphaned children in Morocco.

Larry and Margaret particularly enjoyed having children to come to their apartment to visit at any time but especially at Christmas. They got a videocassette recorder shortly after they moved to Morocco and began to show the children video tapes about Jesus. They knew that this was risky, but they knew that they needed to find some tool to reach the impressionable minds of young children. They would often show the nativity scene from the Jesus film at Christmas. One Christmas they had forty young Moroccans to watch the Jesus film at Christmas. They reported that all eyes were glued to the screen as they prayed that the Holy Spirit would capture their hearts.

Larry and Margaret would go to visit a Berber carpet factory in the mountains at Christmas. They would take gifts to the workers at the carpet factory and try to witness to them. These people of very poor means were always delighted to see them and most grateful for the gifts that Larry and Margaret took them. Larry and Margaret enjoyed a Christmas program that was delivered each year at the English speaking church that they attended. The children of other missionaries who were in the country would perform a musical production each year and sometimes a drama.

Larry and Margaret would often invite friends from the English speaking church and other acquaintances for Sunday dinner. One Christmas Margaret wrote about having seventy guests in their apartment for dinner. Some of the guests were not believers and they would have the opportunity to witness to them as they shared their food with them.

Prayer and Outreach Focus
Pray that God will provide missionaries with opportunities to share the Gospel. Missionaries cannot openly preach the gospel in many countries such as Morocco. They need opportunities to share the gospel one on one. Pray that they will gain the rapport of the people that they are trying to reach.

Chapter Sixteen

Larry's Final Days
Consider the Lilies or the Naked Ladies
in Dublin, Virginia

L arry always loved botany. He spoke fondly of his early childhood when his mother would take the boys on nature walks in the woods and had taught them to identify plants that they saw along the way. He knew the familiar name and the Latin name and species of every plant and tree in the woods. Larry and Margaret tried to pass on this heritage to their young nieces and nephews. They would take them on a walk in the woods after a hearty Thanksgiving dinner and bring back a collection of plants to design their own terrariums.

Larry always enjoyed noticing every new plant and flower that bloomed in the spring. He would gather a bouquet of whatever was blooming in the yard. He would arrange his bouquet with a masterful touch and have it displayed on the lunch table for Margaret to enjoy.

The last couple of years that Larry lived, he was not able to venture outside very often to enjoy nature. One day his neighbor, Don Sizemore observed that a rare lily, the naked lady (genus Amaryllis) was in bloom.[1] The naked lady blooms for only one day each year. Don stopped by to tell him that the naked ladies were in bloom. Even in his frail condition, he could not miss this lovely spectacle of nature. He insisted that Don help him to go outside to see the naked ladies. He talked with excitement for days after seeing the naked ladies about their beauty. Don commented at his funeral that he was now in the presence of the Lily of the Valley.

While Larry was in the Hospice Hospital in Greensboro, North Carolina their friend that had lived with them in their apartment and worked among the Berbers came and spent a week with Jim, Brenda and Margaret in order to be with Larry during his final days.

On one of those days as they went in to spend the day with him at the hospital, he roused up in his bed and exclaimed, "I have a message for you this morning. There is only one way." Margaret interrupted, "Yes, dear, Jesus is the One Way." He said, "Now you be quiet and let me tell it." So he continued, "There is only one way and I am so glad that I went to another country to tell about that way, but now I am going to meet the saints." They were all quiet after this statement. They felt that this meant that the Lord was going to take him soon. He lived three more days before he made his heavenly journey.

Memories of Larry Rogers

by
Harold Dalton, Assistant Director, World Missions Ministries,
International Pentecostal Holiness Church,
Oklahoma City, Oklahoma
December, 2012

My wife, Anna and I first met Larry and Margaret Rogers in 1972 while they were pastoring in Saint Albans, West Virginia, a suburb of Charleston. A few months earlier we were married, approved as missionaries to Africa and began raising our support. We had been invited to their Church and it became a memorable weekend for us in several ways.

At that time when one arrived in Saint Albans the distinctive chemical fragrance in the air coming from Union Carbide could not be missed. That was new to us and we can still remember it to this day. To say the least, it was a powerful olfactory sensation. Thanks to new and improved Environmental Protection Agency regulations that is no longer a distinctive of Saint Albans.

A second thing was that the church was full of children which posed a challenge for us. We hurriedly adjusted our presentation to make it of interest to a much younger audience. We learned the church had a dynamic outreach to children in the neighborhood which was wonderful to see.

The third thing was that Larry and Margaret became lifelong friends. From our first meeting it was obvious they were a loving, committed couple doing the work of the ministry and making an impact in the community. Over the next years we would meet occasionally and have time for short visits. Each time we were in the Appalachian Conference we would look forward to renewing our acquaintance. We also came to know Larry as a pastor who had a strong commitment to missions, always a faithful promoter and supporter.

A good number of years passed. We served in South Africa, went to seminary, pastored in Atlanta, Georgia, then moved to Oklahoma City and took a position working in the World Missions office. One day our Executive Director, Rev. Jesse Simmons, told the staff that Larry had contacted him and expressed an interest in becoming a missionary. This is where the story really became interesting (see letter following this chapter).

Larry had received a special revelation from the Lord. I was in charge of processing missionary applications at the time so I began the normal procedure. This application was unusual for several reasons. First was their age. Larry was born May 22, 1929. This initial letter was dated July, 1991 meaning he was 62 years of age—not the typical time in one's life to begin a missionary career. Second was the people group and place they wanted to go; the Berbers in North Africa where we did not have any existing ministry. Any efforts to minister within a Moslem context can be quite a challenge. Thirdly, Larry and Margaret were both ready to study a new language.

Missionary candidates must take a psychological profile test in addition to a spiritual gifts inventory. Both Larry and Margaret scored highest in the gift of giving. They both scored in the top three for the gift of hospitality. Both of these gifts would be exercised many times over the next phase of their life. Larry also scored high in the gift of wisdom which turned out to be sorely needed with the challenges they would face in the future and in ministry opportunities that would open to them.

In addition to his trip to the local library in Bluefield, West Virginia, both Larry and Margaret became diligent students, learning everything they could about the "House of Berber" including ministry opportunities. At that time in world missions, across many denominations, there was a strong emphasis on unreached peoples with a desire to reach all people groups before the year 2000. In the International Pentecostal Holiness Church (IPHC) there was a program well underway called Target 2000. Part of that was an emphasis on ministry to unreached peoples and in particular the Moslem world.

A young couple, Eric and Becky Watt, had joined our staff earlier. Eric was a graduate of Regent University in Virginia and had worked with Dr. David Barrett, the world's leading Christian demographer. Eric was well positioned to lead our thrust into targeting unreached people groups. We quickly put the Rogers in touch with Eric who began to advise and provide resources. They also went to Pasadena, California to attend a short course at the Zwimmer Institute. This was only the beginning. They prayed, studied, networked, visited and did everything they could to prepare themselves for the upcoming challenge.

One unusual thing that came out of this research was attention on the castor bean. Through a contact Larry had at Virginia Polytechnic Institute & State University, he learned that this particular bean was grown in Morocco and could be used for a variety of purposes including medicinal. He came to the conclusion that he could be a consultant on the development and marketing of this bean. This would give him entry into the country—a purpose for being there—and perhaps the end result would be a benefit to the people.

In 1992 they made their first short-term visit to Morocco. On this first trip Larry visited a university and talked to several people who were interested in developing markets for this bean. An interesting thing was that from his initial conversations the people considered him an expert on the bean. The Lord used this as a means of opening doors in that first period. The fact of the matter is that after much study and many contacts over the next few years the castor bean exploration came to an end because of the drought and it never became part of the continuing story.

It was decided that the city of Fes would be their place of residence, another interesting choice. While Fes is a large city with a population of approximately one million and is the second largest city in the country, it is not a noted tourist destination. Most likely one would have to specifically choose to go to Fes, not just pass by on the way to somewhere. It was also a place of few Christians.

It was a demonstration of divine providence to obtain a residence visa in Fes. The problem was solved largely because of their ages. When the authorities learned Larry was of retirement age they were amazed that he wanted to make this his home. He told them it was a wonderful place and that he loved living there and wanted to stay permanently. They were so glad someone would choose to retire there and had outside income so they would not be a burden to society they granted him status as a retired person. Perhaps that is why the Lord called an older couple!

Larry and Margaret began language study, a necessity to function in a new place, but also a perfect way to build friendships. Almost everyone wants to help a student learn their language. However, language learning is not easy, especially for one advanced in years. This was hard work.

Two very unusual things were door openers for the Rogers. First, Larry noticed that the street in front of his residence was dirty with trash everywhere. He took it upon himself to clean it up. When locals saw a stranger, obviously from another country, cleaning the street and sidewalk they did not know what to make of it. For sure it drew their attention. This resulted in many conversations, new friends and open doors to meet even city officials. A second thing was ministry to beggars. Larry and Margaret were always ready to lend a helping hand to anyone and could always tell many stories of how they were able to make a difference in the life of someone who was truly needy.

A third ministry was to others serving the Lord in Morocco. The Christian community was small in the entire country and especially in Fes. Being a couple with many years of ministry experience and a lot of wisdom they became sort of a pastor and even parents to many others. Lots of those coming through were young single people who treasured those times with a wise, older couple to encourage and advise them. There are many stories of ministers visiting for a short while or a few days in their home going away well fed with new energy and vision.

Anyone who has been involved in ministry in a Moslem context knows that progress can be very slow and tangible results very small. It is a seed sowing ministry, trusting the Lord for the day of harvest to come. For sure the life of Larry and Margaret in Morocco was a seed sowing time. There are countless stories of meeting new people, sharing the gospel, ministering to some need. We look forward to the revelation of the good that was done all of which is carefully kept in the annals of heaven.

Their ministry continued for most of the nineties and the first decade of the new millennium. Age wise, it was for the most part their 60s and 70s. The last couple of years were difficult for Larry. His health began to fail. The good news is that he had a long and fruitful life living almost 83 years. At age 80 he was still serving the Lord in Morocco.

Along the way there was a bit of help from other IPHC missionaries. Phillip and Kelly List served several years in Morocco. Although they lived in another part of the country they did have contact with the Rogers numerous times. A single lady from Oklahoma, Carolyn Fire, was sent to work with the Rogers for a time. Other contact with fellow ministers from the IPHC mostly came during their visits to Spain where they would go every few months to take care of business and have a time of rest and relaxation.

On February 13, 2008 Larry and Margaret were in Oklahoma City for debriefing. All the office staff had time to visit with them and enjoy their company. We took care of a lot of business. Both Larry and Margaret were having some health issues. Margaret was dealing with macular degeneration. Doctors had discovered a spot on Larry's lung. Larry was almost 79, so he thought that their condition was not too bad for anyone at their age. He said he had thought of retirement but could not feel released from Morocco. He had to continue the work God had called him to and soon after they did return.

His health continued to fail and they had to return to America in May 2010. At that time Larry fully believed he would regain his health and return to Morocco. For the next year and a half he battled health issues and ultimately was not able to return, although his burden for Morocco continued to be very strong.

During this time I had opportunity to visit Larry and Margaret on several occasions. His faith remained strong but his body continued to weaken. He would tell me and anyone else from the World Missions office that he planned to return to Morocco. He trusted the Lord for healing and the opportunity to continue the ministry. He prayed fervently for Morocco and for a spiritual breakthrough among the Berbers. In June, 2011 my wife and I visited them during the Appalachian Conference Camp meeting. On the World Missions emphasis night he was able to attend the service although he was quite weak and not able to stay and enjoy the fellowship afterward.

The last time I saw him was October 17, 2011 at the burial of our missionary colleague, David Fannin. Larry came out to the graveside on the grounds of the Appalachian Conference but sat in the car greeting people he knew as they walked by. Anna and I stopped by their house later that day for a nice visit. After

I left it occurred to me that for the first time he did not say he expected to return to Morocco. I remember a good time of prayer both for him and also for the people of Morocco.

At the time of his passing in January, 2012 I was in India so was not able to attend the memorial service but wanted to be there. He was a great man of God. The seed he sowed in Morocco will bear fruit although it will not be until we are all in heaven that we will know the full impact of his life. We do know that the Lord Jesus Christ keeps the record and it was He that Larry lived to please. There is no doubt in my mind that upon his heavenly entrance he heard those words, "Well done my good and faithful servant!"

From the World Missions Ministries office in Oklahoma City we are very thankful to the Lord for Larry and Margaret Rogers. They left a wonderful example of commitment to the cause of preaching the Gospel in a place where the light of the Gospel is dim, a life of sowing the seed in rocky soil where there was not much visible to the eye or to report on statistical sheets. Thankfully, we know the Lord keeps the perfect record and calls each of us first to Himself and then to faithfulness to His purposes. In this, Larry and Margaret excelled to the Glory of God.

Harold Dalton, D.Min.
Assistant Director
World Missions Ministries
International Pentecostal Holiness Church

Letter to Jesse Simmons

1225 Lyndale St.
Bluefield, WV 24701
July 29, 1991

Dr. J. D. Simmons, Exec. Dir.
World Missions Dept.
P. O. Box 12609
Oklahoma City, OK 73157

Dear Brother Simmons;

The portions of your ministry I attended at Piedmont Campmeeting were quite beneficial. Thank you also for giving me an ear to my matter of spiritual guidance. This is my request for application and enter--ing the process to fulfill ministry to the "House of Barbar".

It is approximately two years since I had the visit in a dream. During the intervening time I have given myself to search for meaning and caution in general. I felt, that giving full value to the direction of the angel, there would be spiritual confirmation by others not knowing of my dream.

For information to anyone interested, the dream is as follows:

I stood by a well known intersection near the church where I have been pastor for nineteen years, looking east up Frederick Street. I observed a brilliant cloud moving in my direction. It was impossible t o take my eyes away. As I watched, the cloud approached as a vehicle transport--ing a group of what to my knowledge were angels. Everything was very bright. The"cloud of angels" progressed to the point where I stood and came to a stop. While I observed, one of the angels came down from the group and stood facing me. He spoke deliberately and clearly. "Go to the house of Barber and effect a blood transfusion. This is a people determined on self destruction". I became so fascinated with the face of the angel I was really lost if there were anything else said.

I cannot tell anything about the apparel of the angel or his reentry into the cloud. I was aware the vehicle with the heavenly persons swept away as I stood startled. But my full attention was given to the face of the angel that was deeply marked with age lines. It seemed to me I saw that face for weeks.

After the cloud of angels left I awakened. It was Saturday night. Where was I to go and how was I to bring about delivery from a suicide? We discussed with some about families with the sir--name Barbar. Nothing remotely made intelligent meaning.

I have prayed for months but felt I didn't have anyone to discuss it with. Spiritual guidance has, on occasion, been difficult for me. The previous pastorate of fifteen years and the present were moves because of spiritual guidance. So was my Baptism of the Holy Spirit. But in most cases it always appeared best to refrain from discussing with others until I was ultimately positive myself. So other than a token question with the thought that there may be some additional information or confirmation, I ask about angels having age lines, or what is the House of Barbar? The Bishop gently answered that he could not identify the House of Barbar but he would make it a matter of research. So I started research at the local library. Everything turned to a dead-end. Then one day I asked the assistance of the librarian. To this date she has no knowledge of why I wanted the information or as to my identity. However, after about half an hour of looking she came to where I was with books to say, "I believe we are spelling it wrong. In Websters Unabridged Third Edition, after the word berber came the spelling barbar." Thus the matter opened!

The Berbers (Barbars) are a minority people of the Barbary States in North Africa; Morocco, Algeria, Tunisia, Libya. The people are in all the countries from the west of Egypt to the Atlantic and the edge of the Sahara. They were conquered by Islam and are a part of the Arabic traditions, but are separate in that they hold to a Hamitic language. As you may deduct this research is only begun.

I am certain that your department will have directions to assist us in pin-pointing a place of service to endeavor to fulfill the directive of the dream.

From the few days in Egypt after the World Conference, I question if Margaret and I could be of assistance as teachers with the Egyptian Pentecostal Holiness Church with the view of orientation first hand with the Islamic culture. You may know of immediate opening in one of the Barbary States.

Two weeks ago I dreamed of an English class in an unrecognizable setting. I was behind the teacher looking into the faces of young adults.

There are a few things I note at once. It is not because of piety or spiritual knowledge that I have faced an angel, rather that the Lord has an interest in "A People". Secondly, this whole matter must be directed by the Lord, as was its origin. Age, finances, culture, initial contacts and results demand it. We will await your directive.

Sincerely,

H. L. Rogers

REFERENCES

Chapter One

[1]Allisonia, Virginia http://virginia.hometownlocator.com/va/pulaski/allisonia.cfm

[2]Arbuckle coffee http://images.search.yahoo.com/search/images?_adv_prop=image&fr=yfp-t-701&va=Arbuckle+coffee

[3]Robert Sheffey http://en.wikipedia.org/wiki/Robert_Sheffey

[4]Claytor Lake http://en.wikipedia.org/wiki/Claytor_Lake

[5]1918 Flu Pandemic http://en.wikipedia.org/wiki/1918_flu_pandemic

[6] 1918 Flu Pandemic http://www.archives.gov/exhibits/influenza-epidemic/

[7]Carter Coal Company http://davidgoad.homestead.com/CarterHistory.html

[8]Gary, West Virginia http://en.wikipedia.org/wiki/Gary,_West_Virginia

[9]Martin, George. 1976. Madam Secretary: Frances Perkins. Houghton Mifflin: Boston.

[10]Bright's Disease http://www.britannica.com/EBchecked/topic/79572/Bright-disease

[11]Wearever Aluminum Waterless Cookware http://www.wearever.com/AboutUs/Pages/BrandHistory.aspx

[12]Coalwood, West Virginia http://www.wearever.com/AboutUs/Pages/BrandHistory.aspx

[13]Coal Miner's Pneumoconiosis (black lung). http://medical-dictionary.thefreedictionary.com/Coal+workers%27+pneumoconiosis

[14]Solfege http://dictionary.reference.com/browse/solfege

[15] 2Barker, Edith. May, 1994. Lord of the Harvest. Unpublished poem.

Chapter Two

[1]Rogers, Margaret (no date). Sketches of our Bishop heritage. Unpublished document.

[2]Bishop, Mabel (no date). Unpublished journal. No pagination.

[3] Rogers, Margaret (no date). Sketches of our Bishop heritage. Unpublished document.

[4]Coal mining accidents http://wvcoalhistory.com/id26.html

[5]Rogers, Margaret (no date). Sketches of our Bishop heritage. Unpublished document.

*Miscellaneous quotations are taken from family dialogue and cannot be attributed to any certain individual.

Chapter Four

[1]Holmes College of the Bible http://holmes.edu/
[2]Bishop, Margaret. 2 February 1956. Pentecostal Holiness Advocate.
[3]Big Creek High School http://coalwoodwestvirginia.com/big_creek_high_school.htm
[4]Emmanuel College http://www.ec.edu/about-ec/our-story

Chapter Five

[1]Pine Crest Sanitarium http://www.cardcow.com/288962/pinecrest-sanitarium-beckley-west-virginia/?utm_expid=1016-2&utm_referrer=http%3A%2F%2Fsearch.yahoo.com%2Fsearch%3B_ylt%3D-A0oG7j.5yIVQtT0AAdtXNyoA%3Fp%3DPine%2520Crest%2520Sanatorium%2520in%2520Beckley%252C%2520West%2520Virginia%26fr2%3Dsb-top%26fr%3Dyfp-t-701
[2]Bishop, Mabel (no date). Unpublished journal. No pagination.
[3]Camel, 1947-48. Brown & Williamson archives. http://www.library.ucsf.edu/search/
[4]Lucky Strikes 1930. Brown & Williamson archives. http://www.library.ucsf.edu/search/
[5]Philip Morris 1948. Brown & Williamson archives. http://www.library.ucsf.edu/search/
[6]Cutler, M. (April 14, 1954. *The New York Times*.
[7] Heuper, W. April 14, 1954. *The New York Times*.
[8]Bishop, Mabel (no date). Unpublished journal. No pagination.
[9]Bishop, Mabel (no date). Unpublished journal. No pagination.
[10]Bishop, Mabel (no date). Unpublished journal. No pagination.
[11]Bishop, Mabel (no date). Unpublished journal. No pagination.

Chapter Six

[1] Lifeline Ministries http://lifelineministrieschurch.org/
[2] Woodzell, John. March 11, 2013. Email correspondence.
[3] Ibid.
[4]Ibid.
[5]Ibid.
[6]Ibid.
[7]Seawright, De. August 19, 2012. Letter. Page three.
[8]Seawright, De. August 19, 2012. Letter. Page four.

Chapter Eight

[1]Griffin, Billy (no date). St. Albans Church History. Unpublished document. No pagination.

Chapter Ten

[1]Rogers, Larry and Margaret. December 1991. Virginia Conference Messenger. Page 5.
[2]Rogers, Margaret. September 2012. Email correspondence.

Chapter Eleven

[1]Brussels, Belgium http://images.search.yahoo.com/search/images?_adv_prop=image&fr=yfp-t-701&va=Brussels%2C+Belgium
[2] Malaga, Spain
http://images.search.yahoo.com/search/images;_ylt=A2KJkPzo0oVQsQcA08iJzbkF?p=Malaga%2C+-Spain&fr=yfp-t-701&ei=utf-8&n=30&x=wrt&y=Search
[3] Torremolinos

http://images.search.yahoo.com/search/images?_adv_prop=image&fr=yfp-t-701&va=Torremolinos
[4] Meknes
http://images.search.yahoo.com/search/images?_adv_prop=image&fr=yfp-t-701&va=Meknes
[5] Fes
http://images.search.yahoo.com/search/images?_adv_prop=image&fr=y-fp-t-701&sz=all&va=fes+morocco
[6] Rabat
http://images.search.yahoo.com/search/images?_adv_prop=image&fr=yfp-t-701&sz=all&va=rabat

Chapter Twelve

[1] Collins, Aileen. Jan. 25, 1993. Letter to Marie Hollingsworth.
[2] Rogers, Margaret. March 26, 1993. Email to Marie Hollingsworth.

Chapter Thirteen

[1]Torremolinos, Spain http://images.search.yahoo.com/search/images?_adv_prop=image&fr=yfp-t-701&va=Torremolinos%2C+Spain
[2]Tangier, Morocco http://images.search.yahoo.com/search/images?_adv_prop=image&fr=yfp-t-701&va=Tangier%2C+Morocco
[3]Arabic translator. http://translate.google.com/
[4]Marrakech
http://www.lonelyplanet.com/morocco/marrakesh/images/food-sellers-djemaa-el-fna-square$22523-6
[5]Djemaa el Fna http://images.search.yahoo.com/search/images?_adv_prop=image&fr=yfp-t-701&va=Djemaa+el+Fna
[6]Karaouine Mosque
http://images.search.yahoo.com/search/images?_adv_prop=image&fr=yfp-t-701&va=Kara-ouine+Mosque
[7]Fez or Tarbouce images http://images.search.yahoo.com/search/images?_adv_prop=image&fr=yfp-t-701&va=fez
[8]Jellaba images http://images.search.yahoo.com/search/images?_adv_prop=image&fr=yfp-t-8701&va=jellaba
[9]Kaftan http://www.ebay.com/sch/i.html?_nkw=moroccan+wedding+caftan+
[10]Jewelry images http://images.search.yahoo.com/search/images?_adv_prop=image&fr=yfp-t-701&va=moroccan+jewelry
[11]Leather
http://images.search.yahoo.com/search/images?_adv_prop=image&fr=yfp-t-701&va=moroc-can+leather
[12]Babouches images http://www.shop-morocco.com/hand-made-babouches-46-c.asp
http://ggems.peertopeer.com/
Moroccan music links
[13]http://www.travel-exploration.com/mpage.cfm/Moroccan_Music_Artists
[14]http://video.search.yahoo.com/search/video?p=moroccan+music
[15]http://music.yahoo.com/music-of-morocco/
[16]http://www.youtube.com/watch?v=gkZGi1RdAiw
[17]Mayo Clinic Mediterranean diet http://www.mayoclinic.com/health/mediterranean-diet/CL00011

[18]Moroccan recipes http://recipes.search.yahoo.com/search?p=moroccan

[19]Souk images http://images.search.yahoo.com/search/images?_adv_prop=image&fr=yfp-t-701&va=souk

[20]Moroccan oranges http://www.youtube.com/watch?v=-64FoMx1Ujs

[21]Moroccan preserved lemons http://www.youtube.com/watch?v=ApblfnsB5pE&feature=fvwrel

[22]Dates ripening in the High Atlas Mountains http://www.panoramio.com/photo/63572777

[23]Moroccan stuffed dates http://moroccan-dishes.blogspot.com/2009/02/morocan-stuffed-dates.html

[24]Moroccan salad recipes http://recipes.search.yahoo.com/search?p=moroccan%20salad

[25]Moroccan pigeon pie http://www.cliffordawright.com/caw/recipes/display/recipe_id/798/

[26]http://www.theworldwidegourmet.com/recipes/pastilla-moroccan-pigeon-pie/
tp://uktv.co.uk/food/recipe/aid/514813

[27]Moroccan bread images & recipes http://recipes.search.yahoo.com/search?p=moroccan%20bread

[28]Couscous images and recipes http://recipes.search.yahoo.com/search?p=couscous

[29]Tagine images and recipes http://recipes.search.yahoo.com/search?p=tagine+recipes

[30]Hahira images and recipes http://recipes.search.yahoo.com/search?p=tagine+recipes

[31]English tea images http://images.search.yahoo.com/search/images?_adv_prop=image&fr=yfp-t-701&va=english+tea

[32]Morning (Elevenses) tea recipes http://allrecipes.co.uk/recipes/tag-230/elevenses-recipes.aspx

[33]Afternoon tea recipes http://www.joyofbaking.com/EnglishTeaParty.html

[34]Battenberg cake recipe http://www.recipe.com/battenberg-cake/

[35]4High tea recipes http://recipes.search.yahoo.com/search?p=high+tea+recipes

[36]Victoria sponge cake recipe http://www.bbc.co.uk/food/recipes/victoriasponge_13555

[37]Making Moroccan tea http://www.youtube.com/watch?v=mzVckWest VirginiaTGlU

[38]Moroccan tea images http://images.search.yahoo.com/search/images?_adv_prop=image&fr=yfp-t-701&va=moroccan+tea

[39]Moroccan mint tea recipe http://moroccanfood.about.com/od/teacoffeebeverages/r/Mint_Tea_Recipe.htm

[40] Rogers, Larry & Margaret. March 1994. Newsletter. No pagination.

[41]Ramadan dates http://www.morocco-travel.com/morocco/Ramadan/

[42]What is Ramadan? http://islam.about.com/od/ramadan/f/ramadanintro.htm

[43]Ramadan ends http://images.search.yahoo.com/search/images?_adv_prop=image&fr=yfp-t-521&va=ramadan+ends

[44]Favorite Moroccan Ramadan recipes http://moroccanfood.about.com/od/ramadanspecialoccasions/tp/List_of_Ramadan_Recipes.htm

[45]Aide Kbir Festival http://www.youtube.com/watch?v=3ux_6BA__1c

[46]Moroccan Weddings http://www.ehow.com/info_7944586_traditional-moroccan-wedding-gifts.html

[47]http://tlc.discovery.com/fansites/weddingstory/articles/moroccan.html

[48]http://www.everything-moroccan.com/moroccan-wedding.html

[49]http://tlc.howstuffworks.com/weddings/moroccan-weddings.htm

[50]http://traditionscustoms.com/wedding-traditions/moroccan-wedding

[51]Wedding kaftans http://luxussilk.wordpress.com/2010/11/05/moroccan-wedding -kaftans/

[52]Amaria http://heymorocco.com/culture/wedding-traditions-morocco.aspx

[53]Jabadoor http://www.alibaba.com/product-free/110613968/Moroccan_Men_Jabador_2_peices.html

[54]Moroccan wedding feast http://marzime.hubpages.com/hub/MOROCCAN-WEDDING

[55]Moroccan wedding foods http://www.africanweddingtraditions.com/wedding-reception-food.html

[56]Moroccan wedding lamps http://www.amazon.com/MOROCCAN-WEDDING-CANDLE-LANTERN-CENTERPIECES/dp/B002Q8ATIW%3FSubscriptionId%3D19BAZMZQFZJ6G2QYGCG2%26tag%3Dsquid1420541-20%26linkCode%3Dxm2%26camp%3D2025%26creative%3D165953%26creativeASIN%3DB002Q8ATIW

[57]Moroccan wedding tagine http://www.delish.com/entertaining-ideas/parties/wedding/global-wedding-traditions-morocco#slide-6

[58]Moroccan wedding menus for a week for 110 guests http://macrochef.wordpress.com/2010/06/08/menu-of-the-week-moroccan-wedding-feast-for-110/

[59]King's birthday celebration in 1993 http://www.youtube.com/watch?v=s5G2PnWPSss

[60]Moroccan funeral customs http://edition.cnn.com/WORLD/africa/9907/25/hassan.05/index.html

Chapter Fourteen

[1]History of bullfighting http://www.exploreseville.com/events/toros.htm

[2] History of bullfighting http://www.travelinginspain.com/sevilla/bullfighting_ring.htm

[3]The Plaza de Toros de la Maestranza in Seville http://images.search.yahoo.com/search/images?_adv_prop=image&fr=yfp-t-701&va=Plaza+de+Toros+de+la+Maestranza+in+Seville

[4]La Plaza de Toros de Las Ventas in Madrid http://video.search.yahoo.com/search/video?p=la+plaza+de+toros+de+las+ventas+in+madrid

[5]Plaza de la Maestranza and a matador's suit of lights http://www.travelinginspain.com/sevilla/bull-fighting_ring.htm

Chapter Fifteen

[1] Castor bean project
http://images.search.yahoo.com/search/images?_adv_prop=image&fr=yfp-t-701&va=castor+bean+project

[2]Mid Atlas Mountains http://images.search.yahoo.com/search/images?_adv_prop=image&fr=yfp-t-701&va=Mid+Atlas+Mountains

Chapter Sixteen

[1]Amaryllis http://en.wikipedia.org/wiki/Amaryllis

ABOUT THE AUTHOR

Ravonne Green is Larry and Margaret Rogers' niece. Ravonne's father, Ralph Green was also a minister in the Appalachian Conference of the International Pentecostal Holiness Church and pastored two of the same churches that Larry pastored (the Mitchelltown Pentecostal Holiness Church and the Shenandoah Pentecostal Holiness Church).

Ravonne has many fond memories of spending time with Larry and Margaret as a child when they would come to get her for a visit during the summer or take her to youth camp. Since Larry and Margaret did not have children they were like a second set of parents to all of the nieces and nephews. They never forgot to send a card for a birthday or special occasion.

Ravonne stayed in Larry and Margaret's home in Dublin, Virginia while she was working on her Ph.D. at Virginia Tech and enjoyed visiting with them when they would come home periodically from Morocco.

Ravonne lives in Gainesville, Georgia. She is a professor and has written several articles and books about assistive technology and program evaluation. Ravonne serves on the church board, teaches an adult Sunday school class at the Gainesville First Church of the Nazarene, and is involved in other ministries of the church. She enjoys spending time with her mother, Yvonne Green who resides in Gainesville and going for visits to Dublin to visit Margaret.